LUCK BREAKER

KISMET ACADEMY

SARAH BIGLOW

If you enjoy this book, please consider leaving a review.

For information contact; www.sarah-biglow.com

Edited by: Under Wraps Publishing Services

Cover Design by: Deranged Doctor Design

Print ISBN: 9781955988216

Published by Sarah Biglow: 2022

10 9 8 7 6 5 4 3 2 1

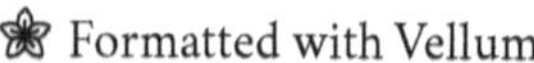 Formatted with Vellum

CHAPTER ONE

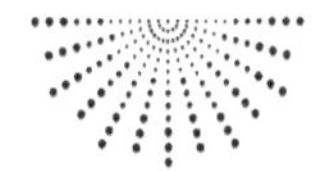

Bashir's declaration that our connection would doom us both hung over me like a storm cloud all summer. I hadn't been able to bring myself to tell *bàbā* about the confrontation with Lee at the end of the semester either. As far as he knew, I'd earned top marks in my classes and been granted another year at Kismet Academy. For now it was enough for him that I could start to pick up writing fortunes for the restaurant over break.

"I have to run to the butcher," he called one afternoon in late August. I was due to head back to campus in a few days.

"I can handle things here," I answered from the back office.

He studied me in silence for a moment, as if

trying to decide if he believed me, before turning on his heel and leaving me in charge. We were between the lunch and dinner service, and the rest of the kitchen staff were busying prepping. Servers were on break, which left me alone in the small room. I still couldn't shake the feeling that *Nai-Nai* was still linked to this place. I'd promised her I would find out who'd killed her and I had yet to make good on that promise. And now, with Bashir popping in and out at random, I hadn't had the focus to even consider what I knew.

"I can feel your anxiety," his voice floated to me, as if carried by the breeze.

I looked up from the tiny strips of blank paper in front of me and sighed. "We've been like this the whole summer and all you can manage to tell me is that you know when I'm anxious."

He gave me a sad look. "As I keep reminding you, we may have been separated by decades, but I was locked in that prison before I could graduate. I am a student, just as you are."

Not a very good one.

Bashir refused to tell me what he'd been up to whenever he disappeared. Sometimes he'd be gone for a day, sometimes a week. Still, even though he wasn't near, I could always feel him out there. I assumed it was the spell that had bound us together when I'd wished him free—the price for my stupidity. In the grand scheme of things, being tethered together didn't seem to be the worst price to pay in the world. For all his doom and gloom predictions, nothing had happened in the three months since we'd finally met in person.

"Are you going to resume classes with me, then?" I finally spoke.

"It is safer if most do not know I am free." He tucked his hands under his armpits.

"Dr. O'Sullivan already knows you're out," I noted. I didn't bring up that Dr. O'Sullivan—now the Head of Kismet Academy—had been involved in imprisoning Bashir in the first place. Bashir still wouldn't tell me what had gone wrong. I couldn't fathom what would have made my grandmother imprison her friend.

Bashir uncrossed his arms and stepped over to the desk. He leaned down over me, but somehow it didn't feel intimidating or overbearing. "I spent fifty years locked away on that campus. I'm sure you can understand my need to be away for a while."

"I do, but maybe there's information there that could help unbind us."

He shook his head, his dark eyes growing hard. "No. I can't be there."

"So, what, you're just going to disappear for months at a time? How's that supposed to help?" I snapped, my anxiety bubbling over into irritation.

"I have been searching for answers on my own. That academy isn't the only place that holds magic."

The mention of some sort of angelic academy resurfaced in my mind. Could a little divine intervention be warranted? In my gut, I doubted even gods could reverse what had been done to us. Not if the rules of magic had any say in the matter.

"What if that's the reason you haven't found anything yet? This isn't just affecting you. It's affecting both of us," I argued. "I may be new to all of this magic stuff, but I can help … I want to help."

His expression softened. "You freed me, because you wanted to spare me from servitude."

"No one deserves to be imprisoned or forced to serve someone else. That is archaic and inhumane."

Bashir's lips twitched into a hint of a smile for a moment. "You have a good heart, Mae Lin." He reached his hand out to touch mine and I barely suppressed the shiver of attraction that danced down my spine at his touch. For all the difference in age, there was no denying he was handsome and the fact we had this strange bond only intensified those features. "If I haven't found answers by the time you finish your first half of term, I promise I will let you help."

"I'm holding you to that," I said, turning my hand over so I could shake his.

THE MORNING OF SEPTEMBER 1ST, I stood in my bedroom, suitcase packed and school uniform already on. While I'd been annoyed at the clothing choices last year, I'd come to accept it as a necessary part of my magical education. I cupped the small stone that would take me to campus in my hand, feeling its familiar weight. I wouldn't say it had gotten a work out this summer, but I had used it to visit my friend Siobhan a few times. Always at cafes or bookshops, never with her family and that was fine by me. My best friend's family weren't supportive of her gender identity. That was their loss.

"Oh good, you haven't left yet," my father said as he stuck his head into the room.

"I was just getting ready," I answered, setting the

stone down for a moment and wrapping him in a tight embrace. "I'll see you for winter break."

He squeezed me tight. "It isn't the same without you here. But I see now that you are where you need to be."

I held the embrace a few seconds longer, then freed myself and retrieved the stone. Turning to face the window that overlooked the street, I held the stone up and thought about my destination. A rainbow erupted from the stone's surface, arcing up and through the window. Holding my suitcase tight, I stepped forward into the beam of multicolored light and left my home behind.

The disorientation I'd experienced last year when I traveled this way had faded the more I used it. Emerging just beyond the gates of Kismet Academy felt as natural as crossing the street. Pocketing the stone, I marched up to the ornate gates with the depiction of a Wisher, a Djinn, and a Leprechaun. It was hard to believe a year ago, I knew nothing of this world.

The gates opened of their own accord and I walked in with the other waiting students. Some faces I recognized as rising third years and others were in my year. I spotted Lani, my former roommate. Our gazes met and she offered a withering glare before turning with a flip of her hair and disappeared inside. I spotted Dr. Shen with her clipboard and made my way to her.

"Welcome back, Ms. Zhou," she greeted.

"Good to be back. I was hoping you'd have my room assignment."

She gestured to a spot over my left shoulder. "Go ask your roommate."

I spun to see her pointing at Siobhan. Her bright red hair fluttered in the breeze as I dragged my suitcase over and wrapped my arms around her. "I told you it'd work out," she said and looped her fingers around my suitcase's handle before I could attempt to carry it inside.

"Maybe Dr. O'Sullivan felt bad about what happened after exams last year and he just let us stay together?" I said as I followed Siobhan to the fifth floor.

It was a different room than the one we'd shared last year, but the set up was nearly identical. I claimed the bed nearest the window and sat down. Siobhan closed the door and rounded on me.

"So, has he shown his face?"

Confusion clouded my thoughts for a moment. I knew she was interested in learning what I knew about Bashir, but she'd never been this hostile towards him. *Oh, of course. Lee.* "No. I haven't seen him since that night. I don't expect he'll be admitted back to campus after what he did."

"He had that ruddy grudge against your family. I figured just because he couldn't get his hands on a djinn to do his bidding, wouldn't mean he was giving up."

I shook my head. "I promise I haven't seen him." I knew why Siobhan regarded Lee with such vitriol. He'd lied to the both of us and used my blood to gain access to the trap that had held Bashir. He'd put both of our lives in danger.

"You know you'd be the first person I told if he did reach out and try to make contact."

I couldn't' tell her that I wasn't sure what I would have done if he'd come looking for me over summer break. I understood the pressure he'd been under to an extent. Living up to family expectations is a heavy burden to carry and it was one that weighed heavier on families like his and mine. Where honor was still such an integral part in how we viewed ourselves and each other. Siobhan's sense of honor and family had gone out the window the day she'd declared her truth. I didn't fault her for it, but I couldn't help thinking it clouded her judgment.

"Anyway, let's talk about something less depressing. What classes do you have this semester?" I said, pointing to the class schedule on the desk beside her bed.

"Looks like Intermediate Alchemy, Intermediate History of Magic, and Defensive Magic. Plus a class on the ethics of leprechaun gold. Ugh, sounds hideous."

I laughed and picked up my schedule. We shared some of the same classes. Although I had an Introduction to Runes class in addition to Intermediate Wish Craft. "Looks like we'll be in most of the same classes this year then," I noted.

"That means I can study off your homework then," she said with a chuckle. "At least most of our classes this semester are practical. I find all the methodologies and background stuff boring."

"I might be more comfortable with magic, but I am the last person you want to try cheating off," I replied, smiling.

Before Siobhan could respond, someone knocked on the door and called, "O'Sullivan's doing an address."

I wasn't surprised. He'd welcomed us all to campus last year and the whole school had been present. It would make sense for it to be an annual start of term thing. As I set my schedule back on my desk, I glanced out the window. We were oriented in such a way that I could see the pond on the grounds below and the crypt that sat on the far side. I shivered at the memory of all that had happened because of that place. I could almost hear a voice whispering my name again, but I knew it had to be my imagination. Bashir had no reason to call out to me that way anymore and the only people who inhabited the place now were long dead. Still, as we left the dorm behind and headed for the auditorium, the tiny hairs on the nape of my neck bristled in warning. I glanced one last time out the window and saw nothing unusual, but couldn't shake the feeling that something or someone was watching me.

CHAPTER TWO

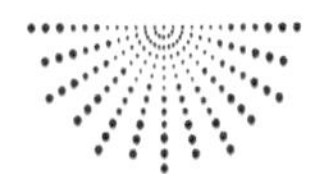

Siobhan and I found two seats near the back of the auditorium and settled in. I scanned the faces around us. There were more new people than I'd anticipated. Then again, I didn't have a good sense for how many students were admitted each year. It wasn't a question I'd bothered to ask Dr. O'Sullivan last August when he'd shown up at the family restaurant to offer me admission. To my surprise, many of the new faces appeared to be of Asian descent. There were more Wishers in our ranks than I'd believed. My chest swelled at the realization that I wasn't alone in my studies. Logically, I knew I wasn't alone. There'd been more than just Lee and I in our Wisher class last year, but he'd been the one I'd spent more time with. He'd been my touchstone to our culture. With his betrayal, I hated to admit I felt lost.

"You've gone quiet," Siobhan noted, nudging me in the side.

"Sorry, I was just thinking that apart from Lee, I didn't really get to know many of the other Wisher students last year. And there are more of them in the first year class than I expected."

Siobhan looked around, leaning up on the seat in front of her to peer at the students sitting around us. "Huh, you're right. That's kind of weird."

A little voice in the back of my head that sounded eerily like Lee reminded me that a Wisher's power only transferred from one generation to the next when the current wielder chose to pass it on. From my limited experience that happened when someone died.

"Guess I've got some new friends to make," I said softly.

"Yeah well don't go making too many new friends. You're bound to make a girl feel a bit jealous," Siobhan teased and it brought a small smile to my lips.

Our conversation halted as Dr. O'Sullivan appeared at the front of the auditorium. Even at this distance I could see he had dark circles under his eyes, his cheeks appeared paler and were a tad sunken.

"Good afternoon all," he said, his voice echoing through the room even though there was no visible microphone. "I'd like to welcome our newest students to Kismet Academy. We look forward to guiding you on your path to understanding and harnessing your unique magic." He turned, as if surveying us row by row until our gazes met. "I trust you have all had a restful summer break and are ready to dive into your studies again."

A few people down in front let out groans. Not everyone was eager to be back on campus. I noticed Lani sat amongst the group who'd voiced their displeasure, but she'd remained silent.

"Before we let you all off to get acquainted with the grounds and enjoy the start of semester welcome dinner, I do need to remind you all that the crypt on the pond is off limits. And we will be having some additional security on the grounds this year."

"What? Why?" a djinn girl with a thick honey-colored braid called from two rows in front of us.

"It's nothing to worry about," O'Sullivan said, waving his hand dismissively. "We're simply doing a security update. It's perfectly routine and happens every few years."

"Routine my arse," Siobhan muttered.

"Why's the crypt off limits?" a guy with bottle blond hair shouted from the far end of our row.

"I'm afraid we've had some vandalism in the past and we've had to place some extra wards to keep people from defacing the dead," O'Sullivan answered.

I doubted anyone else noticed the way his eyes flitted to the left and his hands gripped the podium in front of him just a little tighter. He was a good liar. I knew better than to believe what he said, though.

"Now, I hope you all enjoy yourselves this evening and are ready for classes to begin promptly at nine o'clock tomorrow morning."

I didn't wait for other students to make their exit before I started for the door. Siobhan and I led the pack out onto the grounds. I wasn't hungry and Siobhan didn't appear to mind holding off on getting food right away. We marched side by side to the edge of the pond directly across from the crypt. It no longer held the same pull over me as it had last year, but it still sent shivers down my spine.

"Why do you think they're increasing security on the grounds?" I asked, settling in the grass at the edge of the pond.

"We may not have told him about your djinn tag-along. But my bet is he knew something went wrong in there and he's figured out Bashir's gone. They're probably afraid he's going to come back and get revenge," Siobhan answered matter-of-factly.

"They don't have to worry about that," I noted. "Bashir said he won't set foot back on the grounds, because he was trapped here for so long."

"Yeah, but I mean, he's going to have to come back some time, right? You're linked."

I nodded. "The connection we have feels weaker. Maybe they've already started strengthening the defenses around campus. I just hope it's not able to disrupt the connection completely."

Siobhan arched an auburn eyebrow. Wasn't that the whole point of his doom and gloom proclamation at the end of last year, to break the connection?"

"Don't get me wrong, I want to separate us if it means keeping us both safe. But at least when I can sense him, I know he's okay. Now, I have no idea what's going on."

"Well, we'll just have to do a bit of extra studying on counteracting defensive magic."

I wanted to remind her that I may have taken the introductory classes last year, but I still had far less experience in this world than she did. Also, I hated having to rely on her alone. It wasn't fair to ask her to put herself in danger for me. Besides, figuring out how to let Bashir back in wasn't the only problem facing us. I still had no idea how to figure out who'd killed *Nai-Nai*. My gut told me it had to do with trapping Bashir in the crypt all those years ago. But without him being forthcoming, I had to find other ways of digging for information.

"Guess we will," I finally replied.

Siobhan opened her mouth to speak when someone cleared their throat behind us. We both turned to see a girl with Asian features and a pixie hair cut standing there. She carried a plate of food and gave us both an expectant look.

"Sorry to bother you, but I don't know anyone else and you two looked friendly," she said. She shifted her plate to her right hand, offering her left as she continued, "I'm Ahn-Yi, but most people call me Ahn."

I leaned up and shook her hand. "I'm Mae Lin and this is Siobhan."

"Come on, then; have a seat," Siobhan said and patted the space on the grass between us.

Smelling the array of food Ahn had managed to cram onto her plate triggered my own stomach to rumble. Siobhan and I left her just long enough to get food and return back to the pond. It felt nice to be a trio again. I just hoped this budding friendship didn't end in tragedy, too

I WOKE up the next morning far too early. The sky was still dark outside my window as I rolled over and propped myself up on my elbows. I sat there in the stillness, listening to Siobhan's snores as the sun peeked over the horizon. A tightness in my chest caught my breath as the first sunbeam filtered through the glass, landing on Siobhan's blanketed torso.

Mae Lin ...

The tightness lingered as I heard Bashir's voice in my head. It was far more distant than it was any of the times he'd called to me while he'd been imprisoned.

"I hear you," I whispered to the empty air. I almost wished I could make him materialize in the room with me, but that was never a good idea.

Wishing had gotten us into this mess and a wish always came with a cost. Maybe this would be a small one, like he'd show up naked or no one else would be able to see him, but I wasn't going to risk it.

"What?" Siobhan said through a yawn, her mass of red curls falling across one side of her face as she sat up.

"He's calling to me again. It's faint and it worries me."

"Not for nothing, but he had to be pretty powerful if O'Sullivan and your gran locked him up. I'm sure he can take care of himself."

I nodded even though I had my doubts. Now that Siobhan was awake, I climbed out of bed and started getting ready for the day. I had Intermediate Wish Craft first thing and then I'd meet up with Siobhan for Intermediate Defensive Magic. Understanding how to use my magic for defense might be just what I needed to figure out how to counteract the wards on the grounds.

"Try not to be too grouchy in your ethics class," I reminded Siobhan as we headed to breakfast.

"You can't blame me. It's all common sense stuff. I don't know why they've got to devote a whole bloody class to it. Don't trick people with leprechaun gold. That's it."

"Well, maybe there's some requirement that all

leprechauns have to go through the class to graduate," I noted. It wouldn't surprise me if the classes we were taking now were requirements to leave the school after next year.

"You're not helping with the grouchiness," she pointed out as we got in line at the buffet.

"Sorry."

We found a booth at the far end of the space and sat down. I scanned the faces entering the room, hoping to spot Ahn, but she wasn't among the wave of newcomers.

"So, we should probably meet at the library after classes end today," I said around a mouthful of toast.

"I doubt they'll give us a lot of assignments on the first day," Siobhan noted.

"We can't afford to wait around. We need to know how to counteract the magic they're putting on the grounds. And I need to figure out if anyone else might have had a reason to kill my grandmother."

"If only you had someone you could ask," she deadpanned.

"Believe me, I'd love to … but trying to get him to tell me anything is like trying to get water from a stone."

"Well, it seemed like your gran and O'Sullivan were pretty close. Not that you had much luck last year, but maybe he'd be more willing to chat," she suggested.

She wasn't wrong. It was obvious something had been weighing on him since the summer. I doubted it was just Bashir's disappearance. "Right after classes this morning, I'll go pay him a visit."

As if I'd wished for him, Dr. O'Sullivan appeared in the doorway. He paused for a moment and headed right to our table.

"Good morning," I greeted, trying to act as if we hadn't been discussing him moments earlier.

"Ms. Zhou, I'm sorry to interrupt your breakfast, but I was hoping to speak with you for a moment before your first class."

I shot Siobhan a nervous look before nodding. "Of course."

He took a few steps back from the table and turned his back long enough for me to shovel a few more bites of food into my mouth and wash it down with lukewarm coffee.

"See you in class," I told Siobhan before grabbing my bag and following Dr O'Sullivan into the hallway.

Dr. O'Sullivan was eerily quiet as he led me upstairs to his office. As soon as I stepped inside, he shut the door behind me and said, "We need to talk about your grandmother."

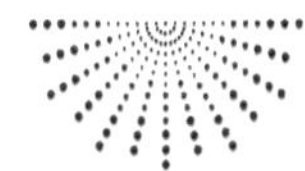

CHAPTER THREE

"Excuse me?"

O'Sullivan rounded his desk and sat down, pointing to the chair in front of me. "Please, have a seat."

The strain in his voice put me on edge. I didn't want to sit, but he'd fallen silent and I suspected he would remain that way until I did what he'd asked. So, I perched on the edge of the seat, hands clasped around the strap of my bag.

"I know that you were not familiar with our world and your family's legacy before we met last year," he began. "But there are some things I need to share with you."

"I'm listening."

"As you learned last year, your grandmother and I were friends during our time at the academy."

"I've seen the photos of you on the wall in the entryway," I noted. I didn't offer up that I knew they'd participated in trapping an innocent man in a magical case for fifty years.

"Well, our final year here, there was a great danger that we managed to avert. Or at least we thought we had."

"What does that mean?" Unease turned to panic and my body thrummed with nervous energy.

"Following your ordeal last semester, we learned that the danger we thought we'd averted, had in fact been unleashed. I'm sure it was by no fault of your own. But you need to know that I have asked magical law enforcement to keep an eye on your family just to be safe."

"But it's just my father and me, and he doesn't have magic." *Not unless I give it to him.*

"It is just out of an abundance of caution."

"And the upgrades to security here. That isn't just because it's time for a refresh," I pointed out. "You think I'm in danger here."

"It is possible." O'Sullivan cleared his throat. "But we believe the steps we've taken will keep you and all of your classmates safe."

"You know that my grandmother was murdered. It's how I received my powers," I said, seizing the opportunity. "Do you think her death is connected to the danger now?"

"I can't say." His gaze darted to the left again.

"Please, I promised her that I would find out who did this to her. I would give her peace. You were her friend; you owe it to her to help me."

"All I can say is the magic that was unleashed last year is volatile and not to be trusted."

Disgust washed over me. I was foolish to think he'd give me a straight answer. "I will keep that in mind. If you'll excuse me, I need to get to class."

I stood and left his office before he could protest. My mood didn't improve as I made it to Intermediate Wish Craft just minutes before Dr. Shen. She gave me a small smile before taking her position at the front of the room.

"Welcome back all," she said. "Now, I'm sure you've been keeping up with your studies over the summer."

I caught the nervous looks my classmates traded with each other at her words. I, for one, hadn't been putting what we'd learned into practice much over break. I'd been too worried about helping my father keep the restaurant running smoothly and keeping

Bashir a secret. If Dr. Shen had expected us to not be rusty on day one, she was going to be sorely disappointed.

Dr. Shen let out a chuckle. "Gets them every year." A collective sigh went up through the room as she continued, "I always set aside my first lesson of the new year for a quick refresher before we move on to the more advanced work on the syllabus. So, for today, I'd like you to pair off and practice a simple wish conjuring."

I turned to my left, expecting Lee to be sitting beside me. The seat was empty and my heart fell for a moment. For all of his flaws, he had been a constant throughout last year that ensured I made it through Wisher 101.

"You need a partner?" a now familiar voice said. I turned to see Ahn standing in front of my desk.

"I didn't know you were in this class," I said, failing to mask the confusion in my tone. She was a first-year student, she shouldn't be in intermediate classes.

Ahn sat beside me, as if I hadn't spoken. "I got my powers a year ago, but Dr. O'Sullivan is very strict about when students can be admitted. I only turned eighteen a few months ago. But my mom had some of her old school books at our house, so I sort of taught myself and convinced O'Sullivan to let me take some of the introductory exams. I passed and he let me join this one."

Maybe this year wasn't going to be as complicated as I'd expected. "Well, I'm glad I've got a good practice partner then," I said, offering a smile.

"I'm sure you're great," she said.

I wanted to suggest that she go first, but she sat back in her chair and watched me with an expectant expression. It widened her eyes just a little and her lips turned up at the corners into the beginnings of a smile.

'You can do this.' Bashir's voice echoed in my mind.

I did my best to hide my surprise at hearing his voice out of nowhere. After all, no one else had been able to hear him when he'd been trapped last year. It stood to reason I was still the only one he could communicate with like this.

I found a scrap of paper inside my bag, a pen from the front flap, and did my best to concentrate. Ahn sat in silence, watching me as I concentrated and centered myself. I closed my eyes, letting the rest of the room fall away as I reached for the heart of my magic. It burned warm and comforting in my chest, like a flame. It grew brighter as I reached for it, letting it fuel me.

When I opened my eyes to look at the girl sitting next to me. I noted a soft glow around Ahn's form as she regarded me. I blinked, in the span of one moment and the next, her face vanished, replaced by the twisted image of the man who'd murdered *Nai-Nai*. Without warning, my vision narrowed to the page in front of me and my hand scribbled furiously, like it had a mind of its own. My hand zipped across the page for several lines before the pen fell from my grasp and my vision tunneled out again, so I could take in the rest of the classroom.

Sounds filtered back slowly. Apparently my body had become more accustomed to going into and out of the trancelike state that happened when I used my magic for seeing fortunes.

"Should I be nervous that you wrote so much?" Ahn whispered, tapping the edge of the paper in front of me.

I didn't know the answer to her question. I never recalled what I'd written in the moment. I made a note to ask Dr. Shen if that was a typical side effect of a wisher's gift. Bending down, I studied my own handwriting: *The truth you seek will be at hand by summer's dawn.*

"I'm still not great at interpreting what comes out. And I'm not even sure I did it right," I said, scrambling to hide the paper away. It was possible that Ahn was looking for the answer to some deep, burning question that would reveal itself by the end of the school term. Besides, I also doubted she could shapeshift into a man capable of murder.

"That's why we're still in class," Ahn replied.

I nodded mutely, my mind trying to sort through why I would suddenly see my grandmother's murderer while trying to predict someone else's fortune. I couldn't just come out and ask if she was related to anyone with villainous intentions.

"Guess it's your turn," I muttered. Part of me hoped Ahn was as good as she claimed to be and she would reveal something helpful. I studied the younger woman as she took out a pad and pen herself. Her tools were more elaborate and I thought perhaps used for calligraphy when she sucked in an audible breath and blew it out. She reached for my hand and her hand turned vice-like around my wrist. I tried to pull free, but she held on tight. Her eyes rolled back in her head as she pressed the tip of her pen to paper. Her lips moved as if she were speaking the words to herself under her breath.

It was over as quickly as it came and she broke her grip on me. She blinked at me and then down at the words she'd written. Her brow wrinkled as she considered my fortune.

"It can't be any worse than mine," I prompted.

She pushed it over for me to read and my heart skipped a beat. *The truth you seek will be at hand by summer's dawn.*

That had to be a coincidence. I pulled mine out to compare them, but the words were identical. "I don't understand," I whispered.

"Something perplexing, ladies?" Dr. Shen's voice cut into our quiet contemplation and I jumped.

Revealing that we'd both written the same fortune was risky. I'd have to admit I likely saw the fortune for someone else without an explanation of how I'd been able to see them. On the other hand, Dr. Shen was an expert in her field and might have some insights.

"Have you ever had a situation where two people who weren't really connected shared a fortune?" I chose my words to be as vague as possible. After all, Ahn and I weren't really connected, aside from being acquaintances.

Dr. Shen leaned over the desk, studying the two pieces of paper. "It is rare, but there are some times where two or more people can be linked by fate and luck so tightly that their fortunes come out the same."

"But … it could be random chance, too, right?" I suggested.

"It is possible." She straightened and said, "You both ought to keep practicing. Try reading other people to see if it happens again."

She had a point. I'd only ever tried to read other Wishers. Maybe I could strong-arm Siobhan into letting me read her fortune just to get practice. Dr. Shen paced through the rest of the room until the end of the class.

"Before you all leave, I'd like to make sure you've received your textbooks for this year. You'll be expected to read the first three chapters by next week."

"So much for a light first lesson," Ahn sighed as she gathered her bag and started for the door.

"Hey, can we keep this whole joint fortune thing to ourselves for now?"

She shouldered her bag and looked at me. "You think there's something to it?"

I shrugged. "Maybe not, but it feels like until we know for sure it wasn't a fluke, it's better to not tell too many people. What's it they say about self-fulfilling prophesies?"

"My lips are sealed," she said and gave me a wave.

I was halfway to my next class when the world began to spin around me. Solid walls were replaced by open air and every nerve in my body suddenly caught fire. The ground rushed up to meet me and as the pain tightened its grip on my body, I could see that same twisted face standing above me, laughing. I could make out the same red aura I'd seen the day he'd come to the restaurant and killed *Nai-Nai*.

"You didn't think you'd get away that easily, did you?"

His laugh echoed in my ears as the pale clouds above me greyed out and everything around me went black.

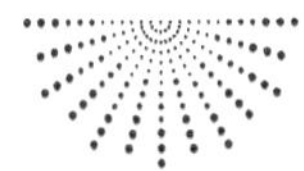

I don't know how long I'd laid there before I felt someone's hands rousing me. I blinked, but the world was slow to come back into focus. At first, my brain didn't recognize the face hovering inches from my nose.

"Take it slow," a man's voice said as I eased up into a seated position.

The hallway came back into focus and I found my bag laying a few paces behind me. I rubbed at my head as it throbbed. I didn't remember hitting it when I fainted, but that didn't mean much. The man crouching before me still didn't register in my mind. He had short blond hair that hung artfully over his brow and startling blue eyes that looked as if they were made from handfuls of crystal clear sea water.

He could have walked off a model runway and it wouldn't have surprised me.

"Sorry, do I know you?" I mumbled.

His features softened. "I don't think we've officially been introduced. I'm Dr. Finn Corbitt. I teach Runes."

I let Dr. Corbitt ease me to my feet. I'd been on my way to Introduction to Runes when I'd collapsed. This was not the way I'd intended to meet my next professor.

"I promise I don't usually pass out on the way to class. I probably didn't eat enough for breakfast." In fact, I likely hadn't given Dr. O'Sullivan's impromptu meeting in his office this morning.

"Well, I'm glad to hear that," he said with a smile.

I stood there awkwardly for a moment before I remembered my bag and bent to scoop it up by the strap. I followed him down the hall and took a right turn, spotting the lecture hall with a smattering of seats filled.

"Sorry again," I apologized to Dr. Corbitt as I walked in and went to find an open spot midway up the tiered seats.

The room quieted down as Dr. Corbitt sat on the front edge of the desk by the blackboard. He surveyed us, his gaze landing on me for longer than anyone else it seemed before launching into his introductory remarks.

"It's always nice to see a mix of students in this class. For those of you who don't know me, I'm Dr. Finn Corbitt. I hail from the great province of Ontario." I caught one girl's hand go up at the other end of the room. Dr. Corbitt spotted it too, but just kept going.

"My aim for this class is to teach you the fundamentals of rune casting. We'll start with the theoretical stuff. I know it sounds boring, but I promise, by Christmas you'll be getting some good practice on theory. Next semester we'll be taking it up a notch with some fun real world practical lessons."

The girl across the room made an indignant sound, unhappy at having been ignored. I craned my neck to see Lani had been the one to throw her hand up. It was no big surprise that she was unhappy someone was ignoring her.

"Excuse me," she said with complete lack of awareness at how rude she sounded.

"Yes?" Dr. Corbitt responded, pivoting on the desk to look at her.

"You're a djinn, aren't you?" she noted and I could hear the hint of pride in her tone.

Dr. Corbitt stood and sauntered toward Lani. I

watched as she sat up straighter. "Maybe it's the Canadian in me, but I find it rather rude to ask someone *what* they are. And it is also rather rude to assume that just because someone is of a particular magical lineage, that it makes them inherently better suited to one type of practical magic over another. So, let this be your only reminder. I will not tolerate insults based on stereotypes. I will not abide questions of anyone's lineage in this class. You are all adults and I expect you to act like it."

I couldn't help smiling. Lani gave a little harumph at his words and sat back in her chair. Dr. Corbitt sidled back to his desk and perched on the edge again.

"Now then," he said and clapped his hands twice. The screen behind him lowered and a projector started running a presentation on the course's syllabus. "I'm not one to hide things from my students. We will have a midsemester exam on theory and your first practical exam will be before Christmas. I will be available for office hours and I highly suggest you use them. You may think runes are an easy subject, but believe me when I tell you that you'll be learning a new language this year."

Dr. Corbitt launched into a short lecture on the textbook before directing us to start reading the first chapter and to prepare a terms list. I heard Lani whine to one of her friends that he has us doing children's assignments.

"Before you can even begin to understand a language, you need to know how it operates. You need to appreciate its syntax and vocabulary," Dr. Corbitt said and sat down.

I opened my textbook and began skimming through the introduction, eager to move on to learning about the basics of runes. As I read, I jotted down what I took to be the important concepts. A rune was just a symbol representing an idea or set of ideas. They fell into different types—offensive, defensive, and restorative. Depending on the order and combination of runes, the same symbols could be used to achieve wildly differing results.

All of that made sense. I tried to remember if I'd seen anything that could have been a rune binding Bashir to the crypt. That had to have been the case, but I was untrained. I wouldn't have known what to look for and I doubted they were still present now. Not that I would have much luck getting into the crypt to check.

More importantly, just writing out runes didn't mean they were active. It required actual magic to achieve action. The opening chapter didn't go into much detail on how that happened, which I suspected was what we'd be working toward in December. If runes were in fact like a language, we'd need to learn the basic conjugations before we could hope to hold a conversation that made sense and worked the way we intended.

"All right everyone, for your assignment next week, finish reading through the first chapter and come up with any questions. Remember, this is all new to you, so no question is too small," Dr. Corbitt announced at the end of the lesson.

My stomach gave an audible rumble as Siobhan and I left the classroom behind, finding Siobhan waiting for me outside the classroom "Mind if we get an early lunch?" I asked offered a sheepish grin.

"Well you were robbed of a proper breakfast, so I'd be offended if you didn't want to eat now," Siobhan answered and led the way down to the kitchens.

THE BUFFET WAS FRESHLY STOCKED when we arrived. I scooped up cheesy au gratin potatoes and some carved ham and beans. Siobhan went for the roast beef and piled several fluffy rolls on top with a pat of butter each.

"Okay, so something weird happened in Wish Craft," I began, digging into my food. "Ahn and I partnered together to brush up on our skills and—"

"She's in your intermediate class?" Siobhan interrupted.

"Yes. Apparently there's some rule about having to be eighteen to enroll. She got her powers a year ago, so she self-taught and took some of the end of year exams to test out of the introductory courses. Anyway, that's not the point …" I said, taking a sip of water to clear my throat. "We both read each other's fortunes. Or at least we were supposed to …"

"What happened?"

"It was all going fine and then all of a sudden I saw the man who killed my grandmother. And that's when I wrote the fortune." I dug it out of my bag and pushed it across the table to her. "And then Ahn read me and she wrote the exact same fortune."

"That seems oddly specific," Siobhan noted.

"Dr. Shen said it's rare for two people to have the same fortune. But it isn't impossible."

"And let me guess, you didn't tell either of them you saw some creepy old bloke when you wrote it and now Ahn thinks you two are linked."

I nodded wordlessly.

"Yeah, I'd say that would freak anyone out."

"That isn't everything. Then, on my way to our runes lecture, I fainted."

Siobhan pointed to the dwindling amount of food on my plate. "Hunger's a nasty bitch."

"No, that wasn't it. It was like I was somewhere else. Every part of me was on fire and I couldn't move. I couldn't speak and her killer was there, standing over me. He taunted me before I passed out."

"You think the two were connected?"

"I don't see how they can't be. Why would I see him and then minutes later he'd attack me. I don't know, maybe he somehow knows I saw his fortune?"

"But you didn't actually go anywhere."

"I … I don't think so, but I know nothing about him. He could be that powerful. The more I learn about magic, the more I'm convinced he used it to kill my grandmother."

"I'm pretty sure whatever wards O'Sullivan's putting up on the grounds would keep even someone that powerful out. I mean, if your Djinn lad is supposed to be so powerful that they're all wetting themselves over him coming back here, their defenses have to be ironclad."

"Wait, maybe that's it," I said, my fork clattering to the plate in front of me.

"What's it?"

"What if I wasn't the one seeing him?" I leaned closer and lowered my voice. "What if I was seeing what Bashir saw?"

"You think you've got some sort of psychic connection with him now?"

"Maybe. To be honest, we haven't really explored it much. He just keeps disappearing and leaving me to wonder. But he said we were linked."

"Say that's true, why would he be off looking for the psycho who murdered your gran?"

"Maybe he can sense how important it is to me? Maybe he thinks if he solves this problem for me, I'll help him find a way to free him for good?

"If only there was a way you could ask him," Siobhan said.

I'd heard Bashir's voice giving me encouragement right before I'd tried to read Ahn's fortune. Had my mind been subconsciously focused on him and that's why I'd seen *Nai-Nai's* murderer? I needed to find a way to get in contact with him, if for no other reason than to be sure he was okay.

"I need to find a way to get off campus for a few

hours. Just long enough to see if I can … I don't know, summon him," I whispered.

Siobhan grinned like the Cheshire Cat. "I think I can help you with that. Meet me on the front steps after afternoon lessons."

I hated to wait that long, but I couldn't just skip classes. That would arouse too much suspicion and if I was going to keep Bashir's freedom a secret, I needed to act as if nothing was out of the ordinary.

CHAPTER FIVE

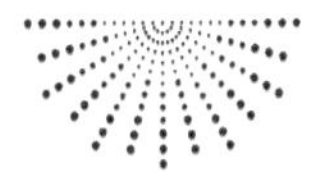

Sitting through Dr. O'Sullivan's Intermediate History of Magic lecture only made me more anxious to find a way off campus so I could find Bashir. He talked about the upgrades to security on the grounds, including passes that would be issued to all students and staff that allowed them to leave and return without being treated as an enemy.

I raised my hand as he paused for breath and caught Siobhan giving me side eye. I waited for Dr. O'Sullivan to acknowledge me and when he finally gave me a nod, I asked, "What's to stop someone from taking our pass to gain entrance?"

I didn't expect Dr. O'Sullivan to smile eagerly at my question. "Thank you for the point of clarification, Ms. Zhou. These passes are a temporary measure we are trying out this term. But … to ensure they are not misused; they are attuned to your specific magical signature. I'm sure you've all noticed that your magic looks and feels different from those around you."

He cleared his throat and continued. "Entry onto the grounds requires not only the pass itself, but your magical fingerprint if you will. And it will measure your fear response for lack of a better turn of phrase."

"You're saying it's going to tell whether we're under duress?" Siobhan piped up.

"Precisely. Simply having the pass is not enough to gain entry. And as it is tied to your unique magic, if someone were to say, try and impersonate you, it would not let them pass."

"But … we're still free to come and go?" I noted, the anxiety that had been constricting my chest loosening just a little.

"Within reason. Students and staff have always been permitted to leave campus as needed and that hasn't changed."

At least that made it sound like they weren't tracking our movements—a small consolation. And in a small way, I could see the benefit of tying the passes to our magic. If it really was as unique as a fingerprint, that made it impossible to change or replicate.

Half an hour later, Siobhan led me down to the first floor and out onto the grounds. I started toward the entrance gate, but she looped her arm through mine, dragging me toward a thick stand of trees and other brush I hadn't noticed before. Had I been so focused on the crypt last year I hadn't bothered to explore the grounds fully? Clearly Siobhan had committed them to memory, because she led me through a well-worn spot in the underbrush and out onto a barren dirt road that wound its way up and over a hill, leading to a small town.

"How long have you known that was there?" I demanded as we stopped at the far side of the hill.

"Since last year. You didn't think I just stayed here all the time, with all of those prejudiced prats?"

"Honestly, I hadn't thought about it. I was a little uh, preoccupied."

"I forgive you," she said and marched on toward the town. "We should be well off campus grounds now. So, whatever you're going to do to try and commune with Bashir, you shouldn't run into any interference now."

That was all well and good, except for the fact I had no idea how to summon Bashir. Every other time we'd interacted, he'd come of his own volition. I didn't like being so out in the open and scanned the shops below us.

"Is there a café or something we can go to? I feel kind of naked out here."

"Follow me."

Siobhan led me to a small café with inviting art deco décor and lighting. They served coffee in tall mugs and handed out free croissants with every order. We found a booth near the back that provided a clear view of the door and settled against the velvety seating.

"Okay, you should have told me about this place forever ago," I accused playfully as I set down my half-empty mug of coffee.

"A girl's got to have some secrets. Now, get to summoning. They're friendly here, but if we dawdle too long it will attract the wrong kind of attention."

Fortified by caffeine and baked goods, I tried to figure out how my connection with Bashir operated. I closed my eyes and slowed my breathing, trying to picture him in my mind while also tapping into my magic. That warmth filled me from head to toe as his face flared in my mind's eye.

If you can hear me, I'm waiting for you. We need to talk.

I tried to conjure an image of the café around us to give him a landmark to shoot for. My power cascaded over me in a heat wave, leaving behind a path of cold sweat as the image faded and the fire within me faded.

"Did it work?" Siobhan's voice was painfully loud in my ears as our surroundings came back to me.

"I don't know."

A commotion outside the café drew several patrons' attention as a meaty thud hit the ground. I was out of the booth in seconds and out the door to find Bashir slumped against one of the outdoor tables. He was clammy and barely conscious.

"I'd say it worked," I told Siobhan as she joined me.

Together we hefted Bashir to his feet and dragged him inside to the booth. I offered up an apology to the barista behind the register and ordered several more coffees and croissants, waving one under Bashir's nose as he gave a soft moan.

He opened his eyes and looked at me. "You are getting better," he mumbled, his head starting to loll to one side.

"Here, drink this." Siobhan shoved a mug at him and I helped him lift it to his lips.

He took a few swigs before sputtering and setting

it down. "What is that?" The concoction had been enough to rouse him.

"Old leprechaun trip. Trust me, it's better you don't know the ingredients."

I pushed one of the croissants at Bashir and he took a generous bite to cleanse his palette. "This one is fiery," he commented.

"This one's got a name you twat," Siobhan replied.

"Forgive me. I meant no disrespect. I only meant that you are a fierce ally."

Siobhan narrowed her gaze at him before standing and pointing to a sign reading 'Bathroom' then disappearing, leaving Bashir and I sitting side by side in the booth.

"Something happened today," I began.

"I know. I'm sorry."

"Why are you apologizing? If what I felt was real, that man tortured you."

"I was trying to shield you from it. I failed."

"What were you doing looking for the man who murdered my grandmother?"

"It seems that he is tied to our current predicament. I admit, I was foolish and sought him out to test a theory."

"You wanted to know just how connected we are," I said.

"I believe we have our answer."

"He could have killed you," I protested.

"If he'd wanted me dead, he would have done so long ago. I fear he needs me alive for something."

"You should know they're implementing new security measures on campus. Everyone's being issued passes tied to their magical signature."

"Well, that won't be a problem, because as I said, I have no intention of returning there."

"But what if it picks up on your magic in mine?"

"You may dislike these measures, Mae Lin, but I believe they may be just what you need to remain safe."

I shook my head. "You don't have to protect me. I'm learning to control my magic and I can be an asset. I told you that I'm going to help figure out how to unbind us."

"Forgive me, I seem to be saying all the wrong things today," he sighed, taking another bite of pastry. "It's just, I fear if I'd been more protective of your grandmother, perhaps she wouldn't have turned on me so easily. I don't want the same fate for you."

"I swear I won't ever let that happen, Bashir."

He nodded, as if resigned to the fact that I was determined to be his equal. Maybe it was a product of him being from an older generation. Whatever the reason, I refused to let it get in the way. My instincts told me the answers laid within the lessons my professors had to teach me this year and in whatever texts might be hidden within the library's restricted archives.

"Do you have a safe place to go now?" I prompted.

He reached over and squeezed my hand in an almost affectionate way. "You worry too much."

"If I worried more, maybe I could have actually convinced you to come back to school."

"I will recover. The food helped," he said and reached for one of the other mugs of coffee. He gave it a tentative sniff before taking a sip. "And so did the coffee. Thank you."

"You have to promise me that you aren't going to go off on your own again. I get wanting to do research, but no more taunting murderers," I said as Siobhan returned from the bathroom.

"You have my word."

"… and no more months of radio silence. You have to check in every few days."

He offered an almost rakish grin. "And here I thought you preferred me to stay out of your head."

"Knowing its coming is less unnerving."

And I kind of missed it.

"I will be in touch more regularly. And you can share whatever it is you discover as well."

I scooted out of the booth to let him leave. He offered the barista a small bow of thanks before walking out of the café and disappearing from view.

"So, what happened?"

"He was testing a theory and it went too far," I replied.

"You two looked cozy just now, you know."

"We did not," I retorted.

"I mean, you could do worse. He's not bad to look at."

"There's nothing like that going on. He went to school with my grandmother," I reminded her.

"Yeah and being locked in that crypt for fifty years seemed to have frozen him in time, because he doesn't look a day over twenty-two."

"Hear me when I tell you, there is nothing going on."

Siobhan threw up her hands. "Okay, fine. I mean, there are plenty of other prospects. Dr. Corbitt certainly has top marks in the looks department."

I wadded up a napkin and tossed it at her. "You've got a dirty, dirty mind."

"What can I say? I call them as I see them and that man is objectively gorgeous. I'd honestly think he's an elf if that were even possible," she laughed.

I didn't bother pointing out that I had no doubt elves existed. After all, if leprechauns, djinn, and wishers were running around with angels and gods, elves were fair game. Would Dr. O'Sullivan bring in such an outsider to teach his students? It could provide a broader perspective on magic.

"And anyway, it's fine if you don't think Corbitt's attractive. That means less competition for me," Siobhan continued, pulling me out of my mental rabbit hole.

"There's got to be rules against dating professors," I reminded her.

She leaned back in the booth and fluttered her lashes at me. "I can wait. We've only got his class for a year."

"You're incorrigible."

"And you need to live a little, mate."

"I think I'm living plenty, thank you."

We stayed at the café for another hour before the barista prodded us out the door with extra pastries. It felt normal and I could almost forget the reason we'd come. But as we made our way back over the hill and through the brush onto campus grounds again, it hit me that this was just the calm before the storm. The connection I shared with Bashir had put us both in danger. I had no choice but to do everything I could to uncover why Bashir and I had been linked, and why I'd seen a killer's fortune that was linked to mine.

CHAPTER SIX

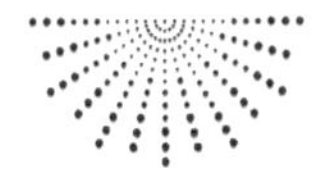

The next morning, Siobhan and I walked into the canteen for breakfast and spotted Ahn already in a booth. She looked up from a book and waved us over. After getting our food, we joined her. It wasn't until I sat down across from her that I noticed the worry lines around her mouth.

"What's wrong?" I prodded gently.

"You didn't hear?" Her gaze darted up from the book long enough to watch me shake my head. "Dr. O'Sullivan announced yesterday that we're all getting those badges today. They're going to be calling us up to his office."

"I didn't realize it was that soon," I said, eyeing Siobhan.

"I suppose he'll feel more secure once it's done," Siobhan noted with a note of disgust.

I didn't say anything, but I didn't like the idea, either. However, there was nothing we could do to change his mind on the subject, so what was the point of complaining about it. As if the mere mention of his name was enough to summon him—was it?—Dr. O'Sullivan appeared in the doorway, flanked by two somber looking men in uniform. I hadn't noticed them around campus before.

"I apologize for interrupting your breakfast," O'Sullivan, his voice so commanding it drew all attention to him. "But I am going to need the following students to come with me to receive your ID badges."

He began reading out a list of names, glancing around the room as he did so. One by one, students stood, leaving their food behind and went to stand in the hall just beyond the door.

"Mae Lin Zhou. Ahn-Yi Chang. Siobhan O'Sullivan."

I turned to stare at my best friend. How had I not bothered to ask her full name? Sure, it could be a common last name, but the way she offered him a withering look suggested otherwise, that there was more than mere coincidence at play.

"You never told me you two shared a last name," I hissed in her ear as we went to join the other students in the hall.

"Never came up," she answered with a shrug.

I grabbed her arm and pulled her a few paces away from Ahn. "Wait … You knew about his connection to what happened with Bashir years ago and his link to my grandmother. But you didn't bother to tell me that he was related to you?" I accused.

She didn't deny the relationship. "Relax, okay? You know I'm not big on family. Most of mine are utter shite and prejudiced twats," she replied just as Dr. O'Sullivan stepped into the hall followed by the two uniformed men. "He's my uncle. He doesn't really like me either, but he at least acknowledges me for who I am."

"That isn't making me feel better," I muttered as we followed him up to the third floor and his office.

"All I'm saying is, he let me come here when most other people would have kicked me out. I don't love the man for doing the decent, common-sense thing, but I'm also not going to shout from the rooftops that he's my family either. We don't do honor and all that. It's better people don't know."

I considered her words and in that moment I

understood why she'd kept it a secret. In all honesty, I wouldn't have cared that she was related to the head of the school. But there were plenty of our classmates who already disliked her simply because she was a girl, and they would have assumed she was only admitted due to that family connection.

"Sorry, I guess I'm just a little on edge," I apologized as we reached the third floor and waited as the other students ahead of us entered his office one by one.

"I know you didn't ask me … uh, and I'm sorry for eavesdropping, but you two were talking really loudly," Ahn interjected, "I won't tell anyone. I get that family can be complicated."

"Yeah, thanks," Siobhan said, eyeing her warily.

Before I could resume the conversation, O'Sullivan's door opened and the line shifted forward so we were standing at the threshold. One of the uniformed men ushered me inside and I swallowed the lump of uncertainty in my throat.

Dr. O'Sullivan sat behind his desk as a woman with a severely blunt haircut that brought out the sharp angles of her cheekbones stood next to an empty chair. She studied me as I took the seat across from Dr. O'Sullivan.

"Mae Lin Zhou?" she said in a clipped British accent.

"Yes," I replied, clearing my throat.

"Wisher," she said, more as a statement than a question, glancing up at me from a clipboard in her hand.

"That's right."

"Right, then. This won't take long." She held out a thin band of silver and gestured for me to hold out my right wrist.

"You said it's tied to our magic and our emotions right?" I addressed the man sitting across the desk from me.

"You won't even notice it's there," he said in what I'm sure he believed to be a reassuring tone.

I held my hand out and the woman slid it onto my wrist. It cinched down to fit neatly against my skin without cutting off circulation. I watched as she sketched a few symbols in the air around my hand, murmuring under her breath.

I hadn't had many practical lessons in runes, but I understood them for what they were. I sat mesmerized in the moment by their beauty, even if I couldn't yet decipher them. The woman's brow furrowed briefly as the runes settled against my bare forearm, but she said nothing as they melted into my flesh, leaving a tingling sensation behind.

"You may go now," the woman said with a dismissive hand wave after the symbols had dissipated and the band of silver around my wrist sparkled with power.

I returned to the hall and waited as Ahn and Siobhan had their turns. I earned a few irritated looks from the uniformed men standing sentinel at the door, but they said nothing. Finally, Siobhan reappeared and took off at a clip. I hurried to catch her.

"It didn't seem so bad," I offered, looking down at the silver band.

"It's just barbaric," she replied, not slowing down. "Come on. We're going to be late for class."

My stomach did flips as we walked into Intermediate Defensive Magic a few minutes later. I couldn't shake the feeling that something bad awaited me within Dr. Wren's class. Not that it had anything to do with our impromptu visit to Dr. O'Sullivan's office. Though the last time I'd actively used my magic, I'd been somehow connected to my grandmother's killer through Bashir. Out of all of my classes, this was the one I expected to be using my powers the most.

"It was a fluke," Siobhan whispered in my ear, as if reading my mind, her irritation of being tracked dissipating.

"We don't know that. What if every time I use magic now, I see him? We have no idea how deep the connection goes," I argued, sliding into my seat.

"And he agreed not to go looking for killers without you, so even if you get a weird vibe from him or whatever, you'll at least not be in mortal peril."

Her words didn't fill me with confidence. I still didn't know how the band would react if my emotions shifted out of fear or surprise. What if I somehow channeled whatever Bashir was feeling? Would it suddenly reject my presence?

I didn't have time to indulge in my fears as Dr. Wren walked in. She looked worn out and the semester had only just begun. I spotted a single band around her wrist as well.

"Morning all," she greeted and settled behind her desk. "Today, we'll be doing a bit of review from last year to dust off your skills before we start exploring more complex magic. You'll be partnered up in groups of two and have to repel your partner's attack."

I started to turn toward Siobhan when Dr. Wren continued speaking.

"To mix things up, you'll each be partnered with the person at the opposite end of the room from you."

I craned my neck to see who that meant I'd be paired with and my stomach dropped. Lani sat there, glaring back at me. *This is not what I need today.*

"Just stay calm," Siobhan urged.

"Not helpful," I muttered as the other students around me began shifting their seating arrangements and pairing off.

I cast one last look at my friend and moved to sit beside my ex-roommate. She let out an audible sigh of irritation as I turned to face her. "This isn't fair. You can't even put up a good fight," she whined.

Maybe it was the stress of not knowing if I'd see my grandmother's killer again if I used my magic, or maybe it was not knowing how to unbind Bashir and I, but her words sparked a fire within me. They were a challenge to show her that I wasn't the girl who knew nothing of her heritage and power. That girl was gone.

I could sense my magic pooling in my core, waiting to be called upon. It bubbled and frothed like molten magma waiting to be released into the world. It had never felt so primal before, but I could barely contain it. I stood, pushing my chair aside and Lani did the same.

"Begin," Dr. Wren called.

I didn't wait for Lani to decide she was going to go on the defensive first. I pulled the power from within me, shoving it at her in a blind fit of anger and pent-up frustration. It crashed into her like a tidal wave, knocking her back on her heels. If she hadn't managed to snake her hand out and grab the edge of the desk beside us, she would have landed on her butt.

"What the hell was *that*?" she demanded.

"I guess I'm not as powerless as you thought," I answered. The anger continued to bubble beneath the surface, hot and acidic.

In the back of my mind, I was vaguely aware of a tiny voice begging me to stop, that this situation didn't call for this much power. I ignored it, readying another wave of pure energy. I could feel all eyes on me as I advanced, not giving Lani time to recover.

I sent a second wave hurdling toward her and she was barely able to throw up a barrier of her own. My magic rebounded and I braced for it to knock me off kilter. Only I remained on my feet. Instead, vibrant green sigils on the floor and ceiling sprang to life, sucking up the power.

"That was not what I had in mind," Dr. Wren chastised, fixing me with a disapproving glare.

The well of anger suddenly ran dry and I came back to myself. My cheeks burned in embarrassment and I bowed my head. "I'm sorry. I don't know what came over me."

Dr. Wren exhaled slowly. "Well, I suppose that's a good demonstration of what you'll be learning this year. Control and moderation. By your very natures, you are all powerful magic wielders. But, as we've just witnessed, you are not ready to channel and harness that power in an effective manner." She clapped her hands and papers materialized on the desks around the room. "Which is why I'm assigning you all some simple breathing exercises and meditation techniques to begin to gain some of that control."

I scooped up the page in front of me and retreated to the desk on the other side of the room where Siobhan sat. Her partner, another leprechaun, darted from the spot and back to sit beside Lani.

"I don't know what just happened, but that was bloody brilliant," Siobhan praised minutes later as we left class.

"I wouldn't say that. It was like I wasn't myself. This anger and rage overtook me."

"You've been holding a lot in, Mae Lin. Personally, I don't know how you do it."

"I felt like someone else was there, urging me to pull back."

Siobhan arched an auburn brow and whispered, "Your sort of flakey Djinn friend?"

"I don't know. I was so caught up in the moment and the fact Lani had been taunting me, I ignored it. And I can't keep reaching out to ask questions I should be able to find the answers to myself."

I pivoted mid-step and turned back the way we'd come. "Come on. I think it's time we started doing that research we agreed on."

The library was a big place, but I had no doubt it held the answers we sought. We just needed to find the right place to look.

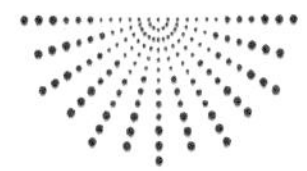

CHAPTER SEVEN

By some small miracle, the anger that had come over me in Defensive Magic hadn't reared its ugly head since. It made attending classes that much less awkward. My outburst had quickly faded into the back of my classmates' minds. Even Lani had let it drop faster than I'd expected. Unfortunately, so far, mine and Siobhan's trips to the library in search of answers had come up empty.

"This can't just be a fluke thing," Siobhan said as we sat in a secluded corner of the library shortly before the end of October.

I closed my Runes textbook and set aside my study notes. "With my luck it is and no one's ever heard of it before. And it isn't like we can simply ask the librarian for any texts on linked magics without arousing suspicion."

"I mean, we could and her suspicions be damned," Siobhan noted with a casual shrug.

I shook my head. "No, whatever there is to find, we'll do it on our own. I don't want to risk getting anyone else involved."

Siobhan let out an undignified snort of laughter. "Oh, I see. You're worried about the poor librarian's health, but not mine."

"You know what I meant. You've been in this since the beginning. And I can all but guarantee you'd never speak to me again if I didn't let you help."

"That's probably true. And that little fireworks display aside, I'm the better fighter anyway."

I didn't tell her that I had no intention of letting her anywhere near my grandmother's killer if or when the time came to confront him. I had already lost one person I cared about to that monster. If I could help it, I wasn't going to give him any other targets.

"You're probably right. And things have been quiet. There's no reason to think we have anything to worry about. After all, that fortune I saw said by the year's end I'd have answers."

Siobhan nodded and flipped open a book on Leprechaun ethics before face planting into it. "This is so boring."

"You can quiz me on runes if you want," I offered.

Dr. Corbitt had already given us the heads up that the midterm exam was all theoretical and I'd been staying up late trying to memorize the myriad symbols with their meanings and uses. Siobhan made a 'give me' gesture with her hand without lifting her head from the book across the table. I passed over the index cards I'd prepared.

I watched as my friend studied the cards for a few moments before sitting more upright and holding up one. "What's this one for?"

I studied the spiraling pattern on the card and tried to recall any of the mental tricks I'd been working on since the start of term. "It's a defensive rune meant to, uh … I think confuse your attacker," I answered.

"Makes them repeat the same action," Siobhan replied. "Maybe I should ditch ethics for this class. It sounds way cooler."

"I doubt Dr. O'Sullivan would let you skip out on a required class," I noted and mimed flipping the card.

"You don't know what I've got on him, but you're

right. I don't need the scrutiny," she answered and showed me a different card.

Before I had time to answer, footsteps approached, muffled slightly by the carpeting in the library. Ahn appeared and pulled a chair over from an empty table. "Did you hear about the party going on tonight?" Her eyes were alight with excitement.

I shook my head, but Siobhan nodded with a smirk. "Right, forgot you're new. Parties here can get a bit rowdy."

Ahn straightened up. "I can handle myself."

"Not saying you can't. But if you get caught drinking underage, O'Sullivan will have a conniption." She paused, pressing a finger to her lips. "On second thought, maybe you should get blasted."

"Don't listen to her," I said. "She's just grumpy about her ethics midterm."

"Oh, come on, don't you want to come? I don't want to go alone," Ahn replied.

"I've got an early morning exam," I countered.

"We'll get you back to the dorms before pumpkin time," Siobhan offered with a devious expression.

I didn't like the conspiratorial glances they shared, but I didn't argue. Maybe letting loose a little wasn't such a bad idea. I'd been so focused on finding *Nai-Nai's* killer and making sure I didn't fall behind in my studies, I'd had little time to just have fun.

"Fine, but only a couple hours. I can't afford to fail this exam," I repeated as Siobhan packed up her books and slid the stack of index cards back to me.

I FELT ridiculous walking out of the building in borrowed clothes from both Siobhan and Ahn. I'd never been one to show off my body. I wasn't ashamed of it or anything, but I'd never wanted to flaunt it. I tried my best not to tug at the too-thin straps of the top or inch the skirt lower on my legs as we followed the markers on the grounds to the path through the trees and off campus. The large tent that had been erected wasn't hard to spot, nor was the chest-aching thump of the bass.

We approached the entrance, paused three across, and shared a look. "Only a few hours," I reminded them as we stepped inside.

Whoever had organized the night's festivities had hung little jack-o-lantern lights along the tent poles and a bubbling cauldron of what smelled suspiciously like apple cider with a strong dose of alcohol sat on a table against the far wall. I accepted the cup of cider Siobhan handed me, but didn't drink. Groups of students stood around in small groups, not unlike the seating arrangement at mealtimes. The bass changed its steady thumping to a more rhythmic beat and a few people stepped out onto the dance floor.

"Let's dance," Ahn called, setting her drink aside and grabbing my hand.

"I'm not really a good dancer," I protested as Siobhan gave me a shove in the shoulder blades before joining us on a corner of the dance floor.

The lights around us pulsed in time to the music and I took a sip of my drink. It was far too strong and bitter on my lips, but I downed it as quickly as I could, letting the buzz loosen my inhibitions. I was allowed to have fun with my friends. I didn't have to be so devoted to my studies and solving the problems heaped on me by the world.

After what felt like an eternity of swaying and spinning on the dance floor, the alcohol made its way to my head, making my temples throb. Siobhan and Ahn were still happily dancing together.

"I need some air," I tried to shout at them over the music, but they couldn't hear me.

I staggered my way to the entrance of the tent and out into the evening air. My head reeled from the drink and I tried to search for somewhere to sit before I fell down.

Someone's hand steadied me, latching onto my elbow, and I leaned into their supportive weight. I had no idea who had come to my aid, but I was grateful. My vision blurred as my stomach churned and I finally found ground beneath my feet. I sucked in air to keep the nausea at bay and looked up long enough to see a hazy face that looked like …

Lee?

No, that wasn't possible. He hadn't been seen in months. And he had every reason to hate me. The figure disappeared as I sat there, squeezing my eyes shut to keep the world at bay.

"Mae Lin," another familiar voice said from beside me.

I cracked one lid to see Bashir sitting beside me. Seeing him there sobered me. "You shouldn't be here. It's too close to campus," I said in one long breath.

He smiled at me. "You are not on campus so I think we are okay," he replied.

I gestured to the tent full of my classmates. "What about all of them?"

"Well, unless Ronan has put up wanted posters all

over the grounds, I doubt anyone inside would know me," he answered.

As my faculties returned, I realized he had a point. O'Sullivan hadn't specifically mentioned Bashir as the reason he'd increased security on the grounds. In fact, he'd not mentioned Bashir by name at all. "What are you doing here then?"

"You forget, this bond that links us goes both ways. I could sense your unease and I thought I could offer some measure of comfort."

"Oh."

"And these parties were rather legendary in my day."

I wrinkled my nose. "Please don't say 'in my day.' I know you're technically supposed to be as old as my grandmother, but it's creepy to think about."

"Forgive me," he said and offered his hand, pulling me slowly to my feet.

"Um, what are you doing?"

He held a finger to his ear. "I believe the music is offering us a moment of calm. And I could never resist a good slow dance."

"I don't really—" I protested as he pulled me close and began to sway.

I said nothing as we moved in time to the music out in the fresh air. The moon hung low overhead, casting just enough light to see by and it caught in his eyes. They shone with a brightness I hadn't seen before. I could see a hint of pain behind the smile he wore as we moved in a slow circle, but despite our connection, I couldn't figure out what lay behind that expression.

"Have you been able to find anything that explains why we're connected?" I whispered as the music transitioned back to an up-tempo song.

"I am afraid not. But I am not giving up," he replied.

"Mae Lin, you out here?" Siobhan's voice rang out.

"You should go. I know most of the students don't know you, but there's nothing stopping the faculty from coming to break this up. We don't need them finding you."

He took a step back, raised my hand to his lips and kissed my knuckles before disappearing into the darkness. I turned and spotted Siobhan and Ahn approaching from the tent.

"You okay, mate?" Siobhan asked.

"Yeah, better now. I just needed some air. How about we head back?"

As we walked back along the path onto the grounds, I felt the tingle of the silver band on my wrist. I had almost forgotten it was there. It flared a bright aquamarine and then faded. A couple of uniformed security guards offered us nods as we headed back inside. As I lay in bed, studying my index cards until well after midnight, I couldn't shake the feeling of Bashir's kiss from my skin.

CHAPTER EIGHT

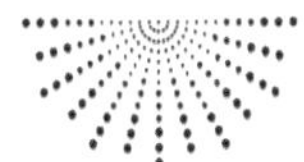

My nerves were a jumble as I walked into Dr. Corbitt's class the week after our midterm exam. I'd spent the week second guessing nearly every answer, even though I knew I'd put the study work in. One night of fun shouldn't have killed my grade. No matter how much I wanted to let loose and enjoy life, I couldn't shake the ingrained need to do well in my studies. It was something I was supposed to excel at. For most of my childhood, excellent grades had been the way I'd connected with my father.

"I know I've been keeping you all in suspense for a week," Dr. Corbitt said as he walked into the room, a pile of papers tucked under one arm. "So, let me start by noting that none of you failed this exam. I'll also have you know, that is a first for me. So, good on all of you. Naturally, some of you did better than others," he continued, walking through the room and handing back exam sheets.

My fingers trembled as I took my answer sheet from him and heaved a sigh of relief at the grade circled in blue pen at the top of the page. It wasn't a perfect grade, but I'd take the A-. I flipped through the answers, noting where he'd docked points. I could build on that.

"At the start of the semester, I told you that after this point, we'd be moving on to the practical application of what we've been studying."

I set the paper aside and focused all of my attention on the man at the front of the room. He looked around, flashing a wide grin. "I'm a man of my word and intend to keep that promise. But we are going to be practicing individually first, so don't get too excited."

I tried not to get ahead of myself as he started drawing runes on the board. I recognized one of them as a symbol of safety. It was meant to provide a safe space for someone to practice in. The second looked like a short arrow pointing upward in two brackets.

"I don't recognize that one," Lani blurted.

Corbitt turned to look at her. "That's because it's the point of today's lesson. It is more of an introspective rune. It can reveal a person's magical lineage. Now, it's perfectly harmless to practice on oneself, which is what we'll be doing today. It will illuminate you in a purple glow for Wishers, gold for Djinn, and green for Leprechauns. Before you begin, I want you to ensure you've set up a safety barrier around your desks. We don't need spells crossing."

Corbitt stood at the front of the room and traced the safety rune in the air in front of him, murmuring the word "*Activas*" under his breath. The spell sprang to life and settled around him, outlining a rough circle about a foot in diameter.

"Simple as that. Once you've all managed that, we'll move on to the next step."

The scraping of chairs on the hard floor filled the room as we all stood and prepared to empower our first runes. I focused, sketching the symbol in the air in front of me. I blocked out the sounds of my classmates working and everything but the image in front of me fell away.

"*Activas*," I whispered and felt a surge of power from my core. It danced up my arm and out through my fingers.

The rune flared bright in front of me and then

settled into a one-foot diameter circle around my feet. I held out a hand to the edge of the circle and found a near invisible barrier had been erected.

"Good. Now, once you've gotten your safety net in place, you're going to repeat the process with the second rune," Corbitt instructed. "Same activation word as before."

Most of us stood silent, waiting for him to demonstrate. He made a "go" gesture to the class at large and settled back against his desk. That did nothing to dispel the curious looks from my classmates. Maybe there was some truth to the fact he was neither a Wisher nor Djinn nor Leprechaun.

"You all have been doing your homework. You don't need me to show you everything," he finally offered.

Here goes nothing.

Again, I focused on sketching the rune in front of me. My hand remained steady despite the nerves I felt making me sweat. I shouldn't be worried about this spell. All it would show was that I am a Wisher. Right? I triple checked what I'd etched in the air against what Corbitt had drawn on the board before uttering, "*Activas.*"

The rune expanded so the brackets encased me on either side. The shortened arrow dove straight into my chest, making it hard to breathe for a moment before the feeling subsided. A purple haze filled the circle around me, but I thought I spotted some thin veins of gold. Panic set in as I tried to wave the mist away, forcing it to dissipate. I didn't need anyone else noticing that I'd clearly done something wrong. I'd somehow found a way to bring out my link to Bashir without meaning to. If I couldn't even hide the connection from myself, how could I keep it secret from those around me?

But maybe there was one person who I could ask that might not ask too many questions about it. As Corbitt signaled for everyone to release the safety spells, I approached the front of the room.

"Good work today," he praised.

"I'm not sure I did it right, but I'm going to keep practicing," I said.

"You should give yourself more credit. I saw that swirl of purple around you. You did it exactly right."

"Thanks." I took a deep breath and launched into my question. "I have a question and I'm not sure you're the right person to ask … but well, I couldn't think of anyone else."

Corbitt shifted his position on the desk to look at me. "I'm listening."

"Has there ever been a situation where two people became magically linked?"

"How so?"

"Like if they were to feel one another's emotions and be able to uh, communicate telepathically?"

"I haven't encountered anything like that. But depending on the circumstances of what was going on when they became linked, it could be the result of a protective spell. To give you a more definitive answer, I'd need to know more about what happened."

"Hypothetically, what if one of the people involved had been imprisoned and the other person was freeing them to save them from their magic being misused."

"In this scenario, is one of these people a djinn?"

"Yes."

Corbitt pressed a finger to his chin before spinning and plucking a sheet of paper from the far end of the desk. He jotted down something and handed it over. "There should be a book in the library that might help."

I looked down at his handwriting, *Wish Granting for Beginners: Djinn Edition.*

"Thank you."

He gave me a smile. "Always happy to help a student's academic curiosity."

I hurried off to the library, finding the book in the reference section and clutched it tight to my chest as I retreated to the dorm. Siobhan wasn't back yet from her Ethics class as I began reading. I didn't have to get past the second chapter before something caught my eye. I read through the passage aloud.

"Like all magic, Djinn wishes always come with a price. If a djinn receives freedom from servitude or bondage by way of a wish requested by another of their kind, neither can be truly free until they can find a third party willing to break the ties."

But I wasn't like Bashir and he was most decidedly Djinn. But those little golden veins of magic that had popped up when I had done the introspection spell resurfaced. Was there something I didn't know about my family?

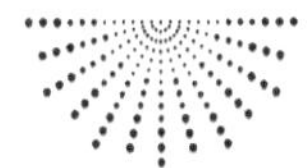

I'd reread that passage a dozen times in the last two weeks as November trudged along, the weather getting steadily chillier outside. I sat in my dorm room alone. Siobhan had headed out early, saying something about needing to get in some extra studying. I stared at the book in my lap and reached for my phone, hitting the first number on my Favorites contact list. The line rang twice before I heard the muffled static of someone answering on the other end of the line.

"Mae Lin is everything okay?" my father said.

"I'm fine, *bàbā,*" I answered.

"It's just that you don't usually call," he noted.

"I just wanted to check in and see how everything was going at the restaurant without me." I wasn't ready to ask him the question that had been on my mind for days.

"Oh, we're doing fine. Still isn't the same without you, but everything here is fine. How about you? Are you enjoying your classes this year?"

"Yes, they are fascinating." Time to broach the topic that might just explain why Bashir and I are linked. "I know I was surprised when Nai-Nai passed her power on to me, but did she ever talk about it with you? Or any magic?"

"When I was younger, she told me that we came from great power, but that we had to work hard to earn what was due us. Why are you asking?"

"So, she never mentioned Djinn or Leprechauns or anything like that?"

There was a pause and then he said, "Not that I can remember. What's this about?"

"Nothing important. Just curious I suppose. I hear my classmates talk about how their magic has always been so open and shared. It got me wondering why ours was so guarded."

"I wish I had answers for you," he said.

"It's okay." I heard voices in the background. "You sound busy. I should let you go. I love you."

"I love you, too, sweetheart."

Gathering my bag, I headed down to the third

floor and found the Wisher classroom empty save for Ahn who sat staring intently at a piece of blank paper. I sat down beside her, but didn't break her concentration. Finally, she blinked and turned to face me.

"Oh, hi." She gave me a wide grin.

"What were you doing?"

"Trying to see if I could force a fortune at random. I know it sounds stupid, but you never know. It always feels like the Djinn and Leprechauns have so much more control over their powers."

She wasn't wrong. "I feel that way, too. It always seems like ours is the more passive power."

I settled into the seat beside her and the *Wish Granting for Beginners: Djinn Edition* book slid out of my bag onto the floor. Ahn spotted it and let out a sigh.

"Still haven't figured out what it all means?"

"What?" I hadn't shared the secret about Bashir with her.

"About how we're linked. I can't explain why, but I got this feeling like there was Djinn magic involved somehow. That's why you got the book, right?"

I swallowed the lump in my throat. She hadn't given me any reason to doubt that she couldn't keep this particular secret. "Uh, not exactly. So, when we both saw that same fortune, it wasn't about you and me."

"What do you mean? Yes it was."

I shook my head. "Last year, I sort of accidentally ended up linked to a Djinn. He'd been imprisoned against his will and I freed him. But now we share thoughts and I think I'd been thinking about him. So, I was seeing something related to him, not you. That's why I took out this book. To see if there's a reason we're linked this way."

Ahn's face fell. "You could have just told me that before."

"I'm sorry. Only one other person knows about this. It isn't safe to be sharing it with everyone."

"Siobhan," Ahn noted.

"She was there when it happened. Not even Dr. O'Sullivan knows what's going on. And he can't."

Her brow knit together. "Why not?"

"Because he's one of the people who imprisoned Bashir years ago. He knows that he's no longer locked up, but not about our connection."

"I could have helped you do research or something," she sighed.

"I know. I just … the last person I trusted also kind of betrayed me."

"Who knew magic wielders could be so treacherous?" she said with a snort.

I couldn't help but laugh with her. "So, this book suggests that when two djinns try to set one another free, they get linked together until someone else releases them. But that doesn't make any sense, because I'm not Djinn. And none of the other people who were there when I released him are either."

But why had my magic been threaded with gold?

"That's probably just one option. Maybe there was some other reason? Maybe whatever spell bound him forced him to link to whoever first tried to set him free?"

I'd considered that myself, but I hadn't worked out a plausible explanation for what that would achieve. Had O'Sullivan and *Nai-Nai* expected one of them to release him later? No, that didn't seem right. She'd warned me about the past in her last fortune to me. Maybe I was meant to somehow fix the wrong she'd caused by locking him away.

"Maybe I have to help right the wrong of imprisoning him?"

"You said O'Sullivan was involved. Maybe you should confront him," Ahn suggested.

I didn't like that idea, but she wasn't wrong. Maybe it was time he knew exactly what I did.

CHAPTER TEN

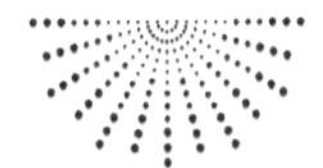

I didn't get a chance to catch Dr. O'Sullivan alone before midterms in December. Whether he'd been keeping to himself or something more nefarious, I couldn't begin to say. But exams had come upon us faster than I would have liked, especially since neither Bashir nor I had any idea of how to unlink us.

Speaking of my Djinn counterpart, I hadn't seen him since the Halloween party and still I couldn't shake the feeling of his arms around me as we danced. As I sat in the library with my History of Magic textbook open in front of me, I couldn't help picturing him in my head.

"Oy, you've got that lovey-dovey look on your

face again," Siobhan remarked, giving my shin a solid kick for good measure.

I winced at the gesture, but straightened up. "Sorry, I just haven't seen him in a while and I'm starting to worry."

"No, you were fantasizing about giving him a good snog," Siobhan answered with a smirk.

I opened my mouth to protest, but held my tongue. Denying her statement wasn't worth the energy. Besides, I couldn't deny there was some sort of attraction there, even if he didn't seem to notice it.

"I need to study," I muttered and turned back to the book in front of me.

I heard Siobhan mutter something unintelligible under her breath as I tried to memorize the facts O'Sullivan had strongly hinted would be on the exam. There'd been a brutal war in the 1500s between Wishers and Djinn, but I couldn't for the life of me remember what had started the whole thing. I flipped a few pages back in the chapter and skimmed the information. A Chinese nobleman had taken a Djinn woman as a mistress, producing an illegitimate child, and when the emperor found out, it had sparked outrage. I would never understand the urge to commit violence simply because two people chose to engage in a relationship. Sure, the nobleman shouldn't have had an affair, but to punish an entire branch of magical beings after he had a child out of wedlock was absurd.

"You going to talk to him after the exam?" Siobhan's voice broke through my concentration.

"What? Who?"

"O'Sullivan," she answered with an exasperated sigh.

"If I can get him alone, that's the plan," I answered.

"You want me to stick around as back up?"

While I was sure my friend would enjoy a potential confrontation with her uncle—one that she might feel obligated to instigate—I knew this needed to be just the two of us. So, I shook my head and replied, "I want to do this alone. After all, he's the one who pulled me aside at the start of the semester to warn me about Bashir."

Siobhan pouted for a moment before her lips turned into a smile. "He thinks he's being all clever, but don't let him fool you. He's scared, because he knows what he did was wrong."

"I will be careful. I promise."

My phone buzzed with an alarm letting us know we had ten minutes to get to the exam before it began. I threw my books into my bag and started for the classroom. I just hoped I could concentrate on the exam.

When he walked into the room ten minutes later, O'Sullivan looked completely calm. He handed out the exam packets and settled at the desk in the front of the room. Taking a steadying breath, I turned my attention to the exam.

Thankfully, I'd retained more information than I thought, because I flew through the first half of the exam. I glanced up at the clock when I turned to the second to last page of essays and caught O'Sullivan watching me. Our gazes met and I held it for a moment. He blinked first and went back to studying a book he'd been reading.

'*You can do this,*' I heard Bashir's voice in my head.

I smiled despite the fact no one else had heard his words of encouragement. If anyone caught a glimpse of me in that moment, they'd likely assume I was confident in my test answers. I hurried through the rest of the exam, grateful there hadn't actually been any questions about wars waged based on illegitimate children.

One by one, my classmates turned in their test packets and left the room. With only five minutes left on the exam clock, Siobhan and I were the only ones left. I waited as she finally stood and turned in her exam. She glanced over her shoulder at me as she left the room and I gave her a small nod. I brought my test forward and handed it over.

"Have a good break, Ms. Zhou," he said, busying himself with stacking all of the exams into a neat pile.

"I need to talk to you," I said without preamble. "It's about Bashir."

I let the name hang in the air between us, gauging the older man's reaction. His hands tightened around the papers and I feared he'd give himself papercuts. A muscle in his jaw twitched as he tried to keep from speaking. Finally, after a solid two or three minutes of awkward silence, the tension went out of his body.

"I suppose you ought to tell me what you think you know, then," he said.

"I know that you and my grandmother bound him in that trap inside the crypt while you were still in school. I don't know why. But he's out now, which you clearly know." I gestured to the air around us and waved the silver band on my wrist. "You didn't take all of these security measures because it was time to upgrade. You're afraid he'll come back for revenge."

"By your tone I take it you don't believe that is a possibility."

"He spent the last fifty years locked up in this place. Why would he want to set foot back here? Even if he was furious with you, which I still don't quite understand how he's not."

"We had our reasons," O'Sullivan sighed.

"What possible reason could you have had to lock up your own friend?" I demanded.

"There are some things you can't fully grasp unless you were there. Bashir is powerful. And that power is dangerous."

"I've met the man. He's no more dangerous than I am," I noted with disgust.

"How much time have you really spent with him?"

"Enough to know I can trust him. He doesn't want to hurt anyone and he certainly doesn't want to use his magic to do anything extreme."

"That may be so, but we did what we thought we had to. And given that he's roaming out in the world, I take it that you freed him?"

"I wasn't going to let Lee use Bashir's magic for his own aims. So, yes, I set him free."

"I know what spells we used to bind him and

freeing a Djinn like that doesn't come without its own risks and costs."

"You know about the binding?'

He gave a small nod, his chin dipping toward his Adam's apple. "I'm guessing you haven't found a way to sever that bond."

"We'll find a way," I retorted.

"I do hope you succeed, Ms. Zhou, but I will warn you, that not everything is as it appears to be. You have gained tremendous ground in the last year with your magical education, but you are still a novice by comparison. Do not lose sight of that."

As I left the classroom behind, a shiver danced its way down my spine, bringing with it a sense of icy dread. He was wrong about Bashir. He had to be.

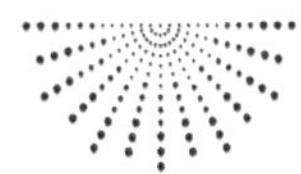

The moment I stepped foot on campus after winter break, I couldn't shake a strange sense of being watched. The grounds were snowy, the pond had frozen over enough for skating for the few brave souls willing to give it a try. And no matter where I stood, I could feel someone watching me. Even when I ventured inside, that unease remained.

"You don't think someone is really spying on you, right?" Ahn said as we sat around a table at lunch in mid-January.

"Wouldn't be that surprising given her little chat with O'Sullivan," Siobhan offered.

"It doesn't feel malicious," I noted slowly. "But it isn't the same feeling I had when Bashir was trying to get me to free him last year. And it isn't the same sense I got when *Nai-Nai's* killer was attacking Bashir."

Part of me wanted to think that Bashir had somehow found a way to get onto the grounds without being detected, but after my talk with O'Sullivan, I knew that wasn't possible. If anything, they had probably found a way to specifically target his magic to keep it out.

"It's probably just me being paranoid," I said, dismissing my own nerves as I gathered my bag. "I need to get to Runes. See you later."

I took the stairs two at a time up to the third floor and found Dr. Corbitt standing in the middle of the classroom, a perplexed expression on his face.

"Is everything okay?" I prompted.

"What?" he looked surprised to see me standing there. "Oh, fine. Just trying to figure out the best way to set up for today's lesson."

"I can help move desks," I said.

He shook his head. "I've got it, thanks." With a lazy wave of his hands the desk vanished, reappearing moments later up along the walls. He gave me a wink and pressed a finger to his lips. "Let's keep that between us."

In short order, the rest of the class walked in and skirted to the edges of the room as they waited for

Dr. Corbitt to explain today's exercise. We'd begun to study protective and curative runes since our return from winter break. It seemed a useful skill to have. So far, they'd come relatively easy to me—at least understanding how they worked in theory. I hadn't wanted to put any of them into practice outside of a controlled classroom setting in case something went wrong though.

"All right, so as we're studying curative and restorative runes right now, we're going to need an injured guinea pig to work with," Dr. Corbitt announced.

Across the room, Lani let out an audible gasp and opened her mouth to speak. Corbitt cut her off.

"Now, I will not be subjecting any of my students to injury just for the edification of the rest of your classmates. We will be working with a magical construct."

He waved his hands in front of him and a burst of white light sprung into being in front of us. It wavered momentarily before coalescing into a humanoid figure. Although it didn't fully turn human, but I could see cuts and other wounds that simulated injuries a person could receive.

"Now, we're going to be working in teams of two," Corbitt continued. "One of you will be providing defensive cover while your partner attempts to render aid."

A few runes on the floor lit up as he waved his hands in circular motions. I didn't recognize most of them. Then again, we were still in the introductory course and there were so many runes we hadn't touched on yet.

"These will be your opponent."

I scanned the faces of my classmates, hoping to find a decent partner. Except everyone hurriedly paired off, leaving Lani and I standing there on either side of the room, eyeing each other anxiously. Corbitt clapped his hands and the humanoid figure in the center of the room shrank, divided, and reappeared with each group of paired students.

"Do you want to be defense or healing?" I asked, trying to keep my tone neutral as I addressed Lani.

"You're the one who can't keep control of her magic. You'd probably kill the person we're trying to save, so I'll do the healing."

"Fine."

As soon as Lani laid a hand on our practice dummy, the air around us vibrated with magic. I couldn't tell what it was, but I knew it wasn't good. I tried to focus and form a plan of attack. Since I didn't know what our would-be enemy was capable of, the safest option was to create a protective circle and hope that held long enough for Lani to do her work.

I sketched the rune in mid-air and whispered, "*Activas*," letting it spring into action. A barrier materialized, gauzy and bluish. Little pinpoints of light zoomed toward us from all sides, slamming into the barrier and fizzling out. It was holding for now, but I could already feel my focus and energy draining with each hit.

"How's it going?" I asked, craning my neck to judge Lani's progress.

"Just do your job," Lani spat. I picked up the strain in her voice.

It was a risk to turn my back on the attack, but I chanced it. I spun around to see that Lani was sitting on her heels studying our dummy with its cuts and other wounds, leaking pale pinkish light which I guessed was meant to simulate blood. The pained expression on Lani's face told me she wasn't sure what she was meant to do.

"Here, trade," I said, nudging her out of the way. "My barrier's about to come down so get ready to put a new one up."

"But I'm supposed to be the one doing the healing," Lani protested.

In that moment, my barrier fizzled out and the tiny pinpoints of light grew larger and whizzed over our heads. Lani let out a yelp before standing up, sketching a rune in the air, and activating it. Her barrier was milky white and almost solid.

"Guess you should have been the defense from the beginning," I muttered and tried to recall the restorative runes we'd been studying.

I had to assume that the wounds didn't carry any magical component to them and went with a simple approach. There was a rune that was meant to staunch bleeding and bind wounds. It would leave scars, but we weren't going for pretty here. So, I traced the rune in the air with my hands, taking care to get the curves just right before activating it. The rune glowed a hazy yellow before wafting down over the dummy like a blanket. The wounds sealed, adding their pale hue to the mix. But the pale pink light dissipated.

"Time's up," Corbitt called.

I felt more than saw Lani releasing her barrier spell and sat on my heels as the rest of the classroom came back into view. It had surprised me that Lani and I could work together, even in a simulated crisis.

"We didn't make such a bad team," I said.

Lani simply spun on her heels and marched back

to the other side of the room to retrieve her bag and rejoin her friends. I grabbed my own bag and headed up to the dorms. As I sat on my bed staring out the window, I spotted the outline of the crypt and that sense of being watched came over me again. I could go down to the crypt and look around, but I knew that would draw too much attention from the wrong people. So, I just added the mystery to my list of unanswered questions. A list that was growing painfully longer by the day.

CHAPTER TWELVE

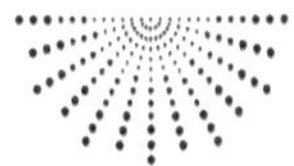

January melted into February before I knew it and I found myself sitting in Defensive Magic just before Valentine's Day. I'd been trying to keep a low profile in class since my outburst last semester. Luckily, it hadn't been too difficult to manage. And after our Runes pair-up, Lani had stopped trying to provoke me. It was a nice reprieve. Also I'd been working up the courage to sneak into the crypt after all. The more I learned this semester, the more I was confident I could get in and out without being seen.

"So, you going to head off campus for a little romantic rendezvous?" Siobhan whispered in my ear.

"Not likely." Even as I spoke the words, I closed

my eyes, bringing up the memory of Halloween in my mind. Maybe it was because I was so intently focused on the memory, but when I opened my eyes again, I was no longer in the classroom.

I stood on a cobblestone street surrounded by squat houses. A shop sign hung overhead in a language I didn't recognize. I moved toward the shop of my own volition and realized that I was not really here. I was seeing things through Bashir's eyes. Could he tell I was here? If he looked in a mirror, would he see my face reflected back at him?

He stepped into a shop. I found it full of gold and silver chains, and gemstone amulets. A squat woman with a headscarf stood behind a low counter at the back of the shop.

"What you look for?" she asked in broken English.

"Protective charms for a friend," Bashir replied.

"You think these help her?" the woman said, gesturing to the shelves around her.

"I never said my friend was a woman," Bashir answered, taking a step back.

The woman's lips parted into a grin with teeth as sharp as razors. Before me, she morphed into the man who'd murdered my grandmother. The man whose destiny was entwined with mine. He rose tall and imposing behind the counter.

"What have you done, Tareq?" Bashir's voice came out of my mouth.

I took note of the name he used. He knew this man somehow. Or had he discovered it in his travels? If only I could communicate with Bashir when we were linked this way.

Tareq continued his vicious grin. "Oh, don't worry about your poor little shop lady, shaqiq. She's fine. Or she will be when I am done with her. But do you really think one of these trinkets could keep your little Wisher safe from me?"

"I am not going to let you harm her. She is an innocent."

"Hardly. She freed you from confinement. That makes her complicit," Tareq snarled, reaching a hand toward Bashir across the counter. "And she is spying right now."

The connection broke and I didn't see what happened next with Bashir and Tareq. I had a name now, at least. Still I couldn't shake the feeling there was more to their interaction. The way they spoke to one another, it wasn't just as enemies. They had a familiarity with one another.

"Oy, you zoned out for a bit," Siobhan said, nudging my shoulder.

"I think Bashir's trying to protect me. But he ran into Tareq," I whispered.

"Who?"

"The man who murdered my grandmother and was torturing Bashir."

"You never had a name before."

"I got lucky. But he could sense that I was there. I didn't know he could do that."

"Sounds like this bloke is powerful. Maybe he's the one we should all be scared of."

"I certainly am," I muttered as I tried to focus on Dr. Shen's lesson on offensive magic. It was little use. All I could seem to think about was the exchange in the shop. I needed to talk to Bashir and figure out what he wasn't telling me. I was tired of being in the dark.

"Well, whatever your little mind hopping means, forget it. If we don't start doing this lesson, Shen's going to lose her shit," Siobhan said, again trying to regain my attention.

"Sorry, I just … I can't focus."

"Just, I don't know, throw up a barrier or something, so I can at least pretend to fight you," Siobhan replied. "She's coming over."

I closed my eyes, trying to push the exchange from my mind as I focused and etched a rune mid-air, murmuring "*Activas,*" and waited for Siobhan to try and breach it.

The barrier was gauzy and I could make out my friend on the other side of it, pulling out something shimmery from her pocket. I tensed as she flicked it sideways at the barrier.

"What have I said about weapons in this class?" Dr. Shen snapped as my barrier came down and Siobhan's throwing star clattered to the floor.

"I work with what I've got. And you should be praising Mae Lin. She deflected it."

"Bring those to my class again and I don't care how connected you are to this school; you'll be out of my class."

That was the first time I'd heard an instructor bring up Siobhan's familial connection to Dr. O'Sullivan. Siobhan ducked her head and retrieved the weapon from the floor, stowing it back in her pocket.

Mercifully, the lesson ended there. On my way down to the first floor, another vision washed over me. It was brief, showing the café where we'd met Bashir months ago. He sat at the same corner table with two coffees.

I didn't bother telling Siobhan where I was going as I snuck through the opening in the bushes and raced full speed to the café. I skidded to a halt outside to catch my breath before walking in and straight to the table where he sat.

"You want to explain how he knew I was there and that we're connected?" I demanded without so much as a 'hello.'

"He shouldn't be able to sense that connection," Bashir answered, gaze darting down to his half-empty mug.

"Well, he clearly knew it."

"I was trying to find a way to protect you from him. If we are connected like you believe, there is only so much I can do."

"From what I hear, you're supposed to be pretty powerful," I said, taking a sip of coffee.

"You shouldn't believe all of the rumors you hear in that place," he said.

"Look, I appreciate you looking out for me. Really I do, but the precautions O'Sullivan has taken at the school seem pretty iron clad. I don't think he's going to be able to get to me there."

Bashir's eyes shone with unshed tears when he looked up at me. "That is not the only way he has to get to you." He reached a hand across the table to touch my left hand. "Whether we want to admit it or not, we are connected and that is something he can use to his advantage. I know we said we would stay in touch, but I fear that I will lead him right to you."

"Then we need to keep looking for a way to break this bond. I mean, what if you, I don't know, grant me three wishes or whatever?"

"This bond isn't like that. It is deeper, bonded by blood and magic, not servitude."

"The only thing I've even been able to find is about when one Djinn wishes another one free. But that isn't what happened."

"I wish I had the answers." He cleared his throat. "Maybe we can just enjoy a few minutes of peace in each other's company?"

I exhaled and the tension that had been holding my shoulders straight slackened. "That sounds nice."

I was getting a Valentine's date after all. We drank the rest of our coffee together before I returned to the border of campus. Bashir stayed on the outside.

"We will find a way out of this. I swear we will," he said before he vanished into thin air.

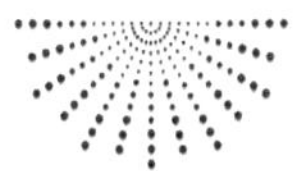

CHAPTER THIRTEEN

The weather started to warm early this year, hitting us in mid-March. The snow vanished and the pond unfroze, casting distorted reflections of the crypt across the water as I sat on the bank. I should be heading to Wisher class, but I found myself drawn to this spot again. That sense of being observed had grown in intensity the last few days and I needed to solve one mystery. It was within my reach and I wasn't going to be able to focus on anything else until I knew what it was.

"Just don't get caught," Siobhan warned when I'd told her my plan.

With everyone else focused on classes, I had an opening to sneak in and see what was waiting for me. I pushed myself to my feet and marched around the perimeter of the pond, approaching the crypt with cautious steps. The last time I'd entered those walls, a friend had betrayed me and I'd ended up connected to a man I was beginning to have feelings for. I'd wanted to dismiss them, but they kept creeping back into my mind.

I'd been putting in extra time studying runes and I'd devised a way to combine both an invisibility rune with the barrier we'd been practicing since last semester. It was the first time I was combining two runes together in practice, but I was confident in my skills. I waited until I was in front of the door before sketching the two runes in the air and activated them.

A thin film appeared in front of me stretching the length of the crypt entrance just as I'd planned and one step down. I bent to study the lock on the door only to find it wasn't secured. I donned gloves anyway, in part to ward off the chill that still hung in the air and to not leave fingerprints in my wake. I pulled the lock free and the crypt door groaned as I shoved it open.

The air was damp within and I held up my phone with its flashlight turned on to guide me into the depths of the space. The fact it housed dead bodies didn't scare me more than the thought of someone living hiding out here. I didn't have to go far before I found evidence someone had been hiding out. A discarded camping lantern sat against one wall. I knelt and felt the side of the lantern. It was cold, so likely hadn't been used in a while. In my flashlight's limited beam, I saw footprints in the dust and trailed them deeper into the crypt, tracing the path we'd taken to find Bashir's location almost a year ago.

"Hello?" I called, before realizing if this person wasn't a friend, I'd just given away my position.

My ears picked up the sound of scuffling and fabric rustling up ahead. I approached with slow steps, so as not to frighten them more. I rounded a corner and gasped, dropping my phone to the ground.

Lee, looking unkempt and disheveled turned to look at me. His glasses were tucked in the front of his shirt and he stopped mid-motion. It was then I realized he was hastily trying to fold up a sleeping bag.

"What are you doing here?" I said, not breaking eye contact as I bent to retrieve my phone.

He stopped packing up his belongings and let out an audible sigh. "I thought it was obvious. I'm hiding."

"In a crypt full of corpses?"

"Where else was I supposed to go?"

"I thought you just went home," I said.

Lee let out a bark of bitter laughter. "After they found out what I'd done, they told me in no uncertain terms I was not welcome. I'd dishonored my family and that it was better if they acted like I didn't exist."

"I'm sorry. That's not fair."

His shoulders sagged and he slumped against the wall behind him. "You should hate me after what I did."

"I mean, it's probably a good thing I showed up and not Siobhan, but I understand the weight of family expectations and wanting to do right by them. In that, we aren't so different."

Lee shook his head. "You are a far better person than I ever hope to be, Mae Lin. Your capacity for forgiveness is amazing."

"I haven't forgiven you," I corrected. "But I understand what motivated you to lie."

"Not that any of it matters now."

I stopped short of telling him that Bashir and I were now linked and how close we felt at times. Or that there was a definite link between the man who'd murdered my grandmother and Bashir.

"You probably could have talked to Dr. O'Sullivan. He would have let you back into classes."

"And subject myself to the stares and the rumors? No thank you," Lee scoffed. "Halloween was as close as I wanted to get."

My brow furrowed at his statements. Some of that night was hazy thanks to alcohol, but I did recall someone helping me outside of the tent. I'd assumed it was Bashir, but could it have been Lee?

"You helped me," I said, jaw slack at the realization.

"Yeah. Well, I guess I felt like I owed you."

"How have you been avoiding all of the security measures they put in place? If you're hiding out here, I doubt you've got one of these," I noted, holding up my wrist.

"I got lucky," he answered.

"No, you didn't. Tell me how you did it."

If Lee could get on and off grounds without being detected, that meant Tareq could find a way, too. Lee fidgeted with something in his pocket, pulling out a small gold coin. "It's a bit of Leprechaun luck. It's what's been keeping me hidden."

"What did that cost you?" I countered.

"Look, I don't know why you came looking for

me, but it's better if you forget you found me," he said.

"I can't just leave you here," I protested as he started shooing me back the way I'd come.

"I'm fine. Like I said, this has been keeping me safe and don't worry about food, the kitchens aren't locked."

"You're going to have to face the world some-time, Lee," I said. "And for your information, I sensed you hiding out here. I didn't know it was you specifically, but I had this feeling that someone was watching me. I'm not that powerful, so if you really think you're hiding out here, you're wrong."

"Just promise you won't say anything," he pleaded.

There was no way I wasn't filling in Siobhan on this discovery. Maybe Ahn, too. But I had no desire to sic O'Sullivan or any of the security on Lee. He didn't deserve that. "I won't tell the faculty where you are," I said.

"I'm just not ready to face them yet," he confessed.

One day soon his Leprechaun good luck charm was going to run out. I just hoped it wasn't while he was in a position where he couldn't protect himself. As I slipped out of the crypt, I couldn't help but wonder what Bashir would think of Lee's situation. The man who'd come intending to free Bashir from his confines and press him into servitude was now hiding away, locked in the crypt by his own desire to punish himself. I couldn't be Lee's savior. I needed to find a way to save Bashir and myself first.

CHAPTER FOURTEEN

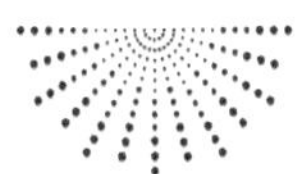

I'd kept Lee's secret for a good week before Siobhan pried it out of me. She'd then spent the better part of March and into April berating me for not reporting him to security or O'Sullivan. Thankfully, after the fourth time I'd explained I had made a promise to him that I wouldn't report him. Though I hadn't made any such commitment to keep it from my friends, she'd stopped asking.

I'd just finished a Runes lesson when my head swam as I stood up. I sunk back into my seat and caught a glimpse of Bashir, except he was younger; no more than ten or eleven years old.

He sat on a dock beside a boy who looked remarkably like him.

"We are going to do great things," the other boy said. "I can see it."

Young Bashir shook his head. "What if I don't want to do great things? What if I just want to be Bashir?"

"You can't just be Bashir, shaqiq. We are going to be stronger than anyone. You'll see."

"Mae Lin," Bashir's voice was older now, insistent.

I blinked, the two boys vanishing and Bashir's image filled my mind's eye. I saw nondescript hills behind me. Although they were familiar enough to know he'd come close to the grounds, just beyond the bushes we'd used to sneak off campus.

Dr. Corbitt eyed me from the front of the room as I realized I was still sitting in the classroom. "Sorry," I muttered and took off at a sprint down the hallway to the stairs.

I pushed out into the springtime air and hurried toward the edge of the campus grounds. I was so focused on my destination I ignored the security personnel patrolling the grounds. Even if they noticed me, none moved to stop me as I slipped through the bushes. Bashir paced on the other side of the greenery, wearing a rut in the dirt.

"You are okay," he said when he spotted me.

"Why wouldn't I be?" I replied, stopping just short of where he stood.

"I could feel him. I'm sorry I could not keep him from your thoughts."

"Tareq, whoever he is, showed me a vision. Or was that a memory of you?"

He hung his head. "It was a memory; one I had not thought of in a very long time."

"Who is Tareq? Why is he targeting you?"

"Because I did not turn out the way he had hoped. I never sought power. I never wanted to rule anything or be in charge. I just wanted to be me. To enjoy my magic for what it was. I wanted to use it to help people. I wanted to make friends. But even that was tarnished by him."

"You're not being honest. Tell me who he is to you."

Bashir's jaw worked as he tried to form the words to answer my question. We didn't need to be connected for me to feel the anxiety and stress pouring out of him.

"He is my brother," he finally admitted. "My twin."

I blinked, trying to let his words sink in and make any sort of sense. The boys I'd seen could have been the mirror of one another. Twins made sense in that respect. But why would his brother, someone he shared such a deep connection with, try to lock him away?

"I don't understand. In that memory, he wanted to achieve whatever greatness he'd seen for both of you. Why would he be targeting you now?"

"Because it became apparent as we grew older that I would not go along with his schemes. So, once we arrived at school, he started plotting. He knew how strong we could be together, but he also could sense that we both had great power on our own. I think in his mind, I was the only one strong enough to stop him."

"So, he had to get you out of the way," I filled in.

"He took the friendships I'd built and twisted them, convincing them he'd seen a horrible future where I turned on them. He convinced them it was better to lock me away."

"But wouldn't people wonder what happened to you?'

Before he could speak again, I realized I'd had that answer all along. The myriad rumors of a dead student could have been born out of O'Sullivan, my grandmother, and Tareq reporting that Bashir had died. And with O'Sullivan quickly installed as the head of the school not long after graduation, he could keep an eye on things.

"Why didn't you just tell me all of this when I first started getting those flashes of him through your eyes?"

"Because I couldn't be sure he knew about you. But, that day in the shop, when he mentioned you were spying, I realized he was strong enough to sense that bond."

"That was months ago. You had plenty of time to tell me."

"Like I told you, every time you left campus, it put you in danger. The more we met in person, the more risk I brought to you."

"I've been learning defensive magic and runes. I can fight to protect myself and you."

"I wish it were that simple, Mae Lin."

"What else are you keeping from me?"

"Magic is in your blood, that much I'm sure you've learned by now," he began.

"It's how we all get our powers, in some form another," I agreed.

"In some cases, blood is power. I could see into my brother's mind as he was laying the spells that bound me. Not soon enough for the full picture to counteract what he'd planned, but it took his blood, and that of your grandmother and Ronan to keep it secured. He was strong enough back then to bind me for half a century. But the spells were weakening. It's how I could reach out to you."

"It was him. He killed my grandmother. When he came to the restaurant, he said something about her giving him what she owed him. He meant blood or magic."

"… and knowing her, she refused."

"So, he killed her. But then if he got what he needed from her, why not come to the grounds and reinforce the spell?"

"Because he needed her living. If I know my brother, he lashed out and killed her on impulse. And he likely wasn't fast enough to take your blood when she passed the magic to you."

My head spun from the deluge of information and I sunk to the ground. I massaged my temples and refused to look at the man standing before me.

"You have every right to be furious with me," he said.

"I don't need you to tell me how to feel," I snapped. "You both see me as a weak, incapable woman."

"That is the farthest thing from the truth," he said, bending down to my level. "I find myself caring for you more than I ever expected or thought possible. If I had to be bound to anyone, I am grateful it is you."

"Why?"

"Because you have a strong will and a profound sense of justice. You will fight to protect all, even those who have wronged you, because it is the right thing to do. I know that we fill find an answer to breaking this bond. Although sometimes I question whether it would be foolish to do so. I wonder if perhaps fate has linked us in this way for a reason."

"I'm still pissed at you. But you have a point. We can use the bond to our advantage. We need to start coming up with a plan to lure Tareq to us. We know that he won't be able to resist coming after both of us. But we're going to do it on our terms and control everything we can."

What that would look like I had no idea and only hoped it would come to me before time ran out.

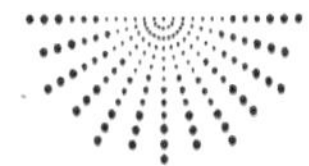

CHAPTER FIFTEEN

Despite having more of the pieces to this puzzle, I hadn't managed to formulate any sort of plan on how to confront or stop Tareq from doing whatever it was he planned. Not that Bashir had been forthcoming if he knew that information, too. I'd spent most of the last few weeks throwing myself into my studies, preferring to focus on things I could actually control.

"You just say the word and I'll beat that man's arse for you," Siobhan offered for the millionth time as we sat sequestered in a back corner of the library.

"I'm not usually one for violence, but I agree. He broke your trust," Ahn said from her spot up against the back wall.

"I'm furious with him for keeping it from me, but

there's a part of me that understands why he did it," I groaned, flopping onto the pile of books in front of me.

"Don't let his charm get in your head. He withheld vital information, nuggets you could have used," Siobhan railed.

"But even though I know the information now, how does it help us? We're no closer to figuring out what to do or how to even take his brother on." I banged my head against the front cover of my Runes textbook. "He's far more powerful than I am and to be honest I haven't seen Bashir actively use magic to defend himself. In that first vision I had last semester, he wasn't fighting back."

"You've got more power than you think," Ahn said in a tone that suggested she was trying to butter me up.

"I appreciate that, but objectively it isn't true. I've had a few bursts of power when I've gotten emotional. That isn't what I'd call an asset."

"You're right pissed about the whole bloody situation," Siobhan noted. "Use that. If you happen to just explode, magically speaking, in that prat's vicinity, all the better."

"What if that's what he wants, for me to lose

control? I couldn't guarantee I wouldn't hurt Bashir in the process," I countered.

"You've been studying runes all year, what if you cast some sort of protection on him?" Ahn suggested.

It wasn't a bad idea. We'd gone through most of the basic runes at this point and I had been marking ones I thought might be handy in a fight. But I hadn't seen ones specifically to protect someone from attack. *That doesn't mean you can't create one.*

Or maybe I didn't need runes. Maybe I just needed a bit of luck. I wasn't going to take Lee's bit of protection from him, but it did give me an idea. I sat up and looked across the table at my roommate. "Have you ever doled out Leprechaun's luck?"

Siobhan wrinkled her nose. "Nope. And as this sodding ethics class has drilled into my head all year, that's about the worst thing you can give a person."

"Why?"

"Its price is exacting and cruel. It gives you luck, sure … and usually it's the good kind, but it takes the luck from the people you care about. The people you love most."

Why had Lee accepted such a thing? As a way to get back at the family who'd shunned him after he'd come home seeking redemption. What sort of bad luck had befallen them without him knowing?

"Is that the sort of thing you'd tell someone up front if they came to you asking?" I probed.

"If you're a decent person, yeah. You always want people to make informed decisions when dealing with Leprechaun magic. It's always just so damn finnicky. Where'd you even hear about it?"

"Lee," I murmured.

We'd managed to go a good month without her threatening to march down to the crypt and give him a piece of her mind, and likely her fist. Her gaze sharpened at his name, but she said nothing.

"Isn't that the guy who tried to use Bashir last year?" Ahn remarked in a conversational tone.

"Yes. I don't know if he's aware of the price he's paying to keep himself hidden."

"That boy was always too clever for his own good. If the idiot who gave him a piece of Leprechaun luck didn't fill him in on the details, you can bet he figured it out himself. And didn't give a shite about it."

Before I could formulate a response, the shelves of neatly cataloged books wavered in my field of vision. I braced for some taunt from Tareq, but instead I saw the café that had become our rendezvous spot. The vision passed and I sucked in a breath.

"Bashir wants to meet," I told my friends.

"You aren't going alone," Siobhan replied, starting to shovel her books into her bag.

"Until we have a solid plan of what comes next, it's safer if you aren't there. I couldn't live with myself if something happened to either of you. Bashir had a point about keeping our meetings infrequent. It gives Tareq fewer chances to get us both in one place at once."

I gathered my books, cast my friends an apologetic look, and headed down to the entrance of the building. I spotted Dr. Corbitt coming in as I was leaving.

"Afternoon," he greeted with a small smile. "Nice afternoon for some outdoor studying."

My cheeks warmed with embarrassment. "Yeah, it is. I've got to be ready for that final next week," I answered and patted my bag.

"Something tells me you're not going to have any trouble passing," he said cheerily before stepping back inside.

At least someone had faith in my abilities. I hurried along the open grassy expanse by the pond before I ducked through the bushes and trudged down the hill to the café. This time, no coffee waited for me when I sat down across from Bashir. Stress had drawn the skin around his eyes tight and he looked tired.

"I'm still mad at you," I noted.

"He's been sending me visions," he said rubbing at the nape of his neck. "Most of the time I can tell they aren't real, but sometimes it's harder to know the difference."

"What does he want? If he wanted you out of the way, why didn't he just kill you?"

Bashir let out a bitter laugh. "Because my brother is all about sport and competition. I think despite everything, he sees me as his only worthy adversary and where would the fun be in killing me?"

"Then what is the point of it all?"

"To show me that he's amassed more power in the fifty years I've been locked away."

"Then we need to find a way to boost your power and we need to draw him out ... Somewhere we can control."

"I agree, but I hate to admit I am at a loss of where that higher ground is."

"The crypt," I said before realizing I'd had the thought. "It's where all of this has gone down so far. It seems as fitting a place as any."

"While it would be symbolic, he knows that place. No, we are going to need somewhere out in the open and away from innocents. I know my brother and he will try to inflict as much damage on those he deems collateral damage."

"Unless you want to lure him to a desert, I don't see any other options."

"I just don't like putting everyone on campus in danger."

"What if I warned O'Sullivan about it, got him to keep everyone inside or end the semester early?"

"Ronan would never disrupt the school like that and we can't be sure Tareq doesn't still have sway over him."

"The fields just beyond the school then? It's not populated and I'm sure we can find a way to confine the damage."

"He is growing impatient."

"Hold him off for another week if you can. Once exams are over, maybe people will start leaving campus on their own and we won't have to worry about them," I suggested.

Bashir's shoulders tensed, but he nodded. "I will see what I can do."

It would also give me time to make sure I had the

right set of runes in place to try and keep everyone else safe.

"I know you are still angry. But I can only apologize so many times for my actions. If we are going into this together, we cannot give him any way to turn us on each other," Bashir said as I started to stand up.

I sunk back into the seat. "I understand why you kept it from me. But I can't just forgive you because it's convenient. I would have thought that your connection to my family and to me specifically would have made you realize that keeping secrets from me never works out like you planned."

He reached a hand across the table to grip mine. "I know. Feeling your pain has been worse than anything my brother could inflict on me. But we must be united when we face him."

"We will be," I answered and pulled my hand free.

Time to set our trap.

CHAPTER SIXTEEN

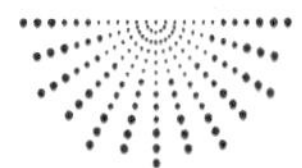

By the next week, I'd spent every waking moment pouring over both my Runes and Defensive Magic textbooks, trying to find anything I could use to protect Bashir and everyone else from whatever chaos Tareq sought to unleash. Now I could recite most of the textbook as I walked into the Runes final exam.

Dr. Corbitt stood in the front of the room and I noted fresh runes etched out on the floor all around the classroom in a repeating pattern. I recognized them as confinement runes, meant to keep magic in one localized space. The fact that they repeated suggested we'd each be performing practical skills. I settled into one segment near the back of the room. Mentally, I recited the most common runes used for healing and restoration, followed by the ones best suited for defensive magic. The rest of the class filtered in and I watched as Dr. Corbitt tapped the board with his right index finger. A series of runes appeared on the board in what appeared to be random order.

"Your task is to determine what each of these runes are and how they fit together. You'll have two hours," he said. "Starting now."

A digital display appeared at the top of the board, counting down the time left. He waved a hand and the runes on the floor blazed a vibrant orange hue. I could feel the confinement barrier as I stuck my hand out in front of me. It was almost rubbery in texture as I pulled my fingers away and studied the four runes written on the board.

I recognized each of them in turn. The first two were ones I'd used to sneak into the crypt without being seen. The third appeared to be something like a shield and the final looked to represent a lock.

Maybe it was because my mind had been so focused on finding ways to protect people that I spotted it so quickly. I had the pieces to allow someone to make an approach unseen and defend themselves. I wasn't entirely sure about the locking rune, but I could sort that out later.

I raised my hands and etched the first two runes together, but stopped short of activating them. Being invisible was all well and good, but if you didn't have the protection rune to afford that extra layer of security, then not being seen seemed foolish. I swiped my hands through what I'd sketched and the symbols vanished. Starting with the shield rune, I whispered, *"Activas,"* and it grew to cover me from head to toe, wrapping around me like armor. I still had the freedom to move as I wanted, but I could still sense the magic at work, hardening every joint against attack.

I moved on to the invisibility portion of the spell. I felt it drape over me, but the moment I moved, the spell slid away, leaving me exposed.

"So that's what the lock is for," I muttered.

I tried to channel the invisibility spell into the ground to burn it out, but the confinement runes around me burned brighter, keeping the magic active. I had no choice but to try the spell again and hope that layering another level of invisibility on top of the one I'd already created wouldn't have some strange reaction. I etched the lock rune first, studying it up close. It appeared incomplete even though I copied it exactly as Dr. Corbitt had drawn it on the board. When I redrew the invisibility rune beside it, I could see where they met. I wiped the two runes away, understanding what I needed to do now.

I sketched the lock rune in mid-air and immediately went into drawing the invisibility rune. Swallowing back my nerves, I said, *"Activas."* The spell ignited a blinding shade of green and draped over me. I held up a hand to my face once my vision cleared and couldn't make out even the faint outline of my fingers. I'd done it.

Around me, the confine runes sparked and released the magic I'd been using. They were clearly more than confinement runes as they sucked up the spells I'd been throwing around and my hand came back into view. The timer at the top of the board read twenty minutes had passed. It hadn't felt like I'd been focusing on the task that long.

I turned and my gaze met Dr. Corbitt's. He nodded, pointing to the door, and mimed opening it. I was free to go. I retrieved my bag and headed into the hallway, exhaling as I did so. Whether he knew it or not, Dr. Corbitt had given me exactly what I needed to face off against Tareq.

I didn't have time to celebrate that revelation, though, because I had my last final exam—Wish Craft. I spotted Ahn standing outside the classroom studying a page of notes. She looked up when I tapped her on the shoulder.

"How'd your Runes exam go?" she asked.

"Good, I think. And it gave me some ideas on how to approach the Tareq problem," I answered with a grin.

"I just hope Dr. Shen doesn't throw too much at us today. I don't know why, but I'm feeling nervous," Ahn replied.

"You've been studying for this exam all week. You're going to ace it," I reassured her. "Besides, there's only so much studying we can do before we either know the material or we don't."

She nodded as Dr. Shen opened the door and ushered us in. I sat down at one of the desks and tried to take a calming breath. Bashir had been keeping Tareq out of my head. I just needed to make it through this next two hours and I could turn my attention to facing *Nai-Nai's* killer.

"Today's exam is broken up into two parts. A written exam and a practical exam," Dr. Shen announced as she clapped her hands once and papers appeared in front of us.

I picked up my pen and started scanning the questions. Right before the end of semester, we'd covered a brief section on the ethics of doling out fortunes and a lot of the questions seemed focused on that. Most of the answers felt more like common sense and I second guessed a few of my answers before Dr. Shen clapped her hands again, signaling time was up for the written portion of the exam.

"Your practical exam will be to see the fortune of another classmate," Dr. Shen announced. Slips of paper appeared on the desks in front of us along with a single sheet of blank paper and a pen to write down whatever we saw.

I turned mine over and was relieved to see Ahn's name there. Maybe this time I'd actually see something about her future, instead of some dire vision related to Bashir and Tareq.

Dr. Shen gave us no more guidance than that as she sat down and left us to our own devices. I assumed we were supposed to try and focus on our subject, connecting to them. I said a silent prayer that she'd also gotten me, because otherwise, most of my classmates didn't know me. I doubted they'd successfully see anything about my future. Then again, they might think they'd done something wrong if it had anything do with the impending fight with Tareq.

I closed my eyes, pressing my left hand to the sheet with Ahn's name written on it. I pictured her in my mind's eye. Her bright smile and bubbling excitement to be here studying in these halls. I could feel my magic uncoil itself in my chest, ready to do as I bid it.

This felt natural, peeking into the future of other people's lives to help guide their fates. While I enjoyed the other ways I'd learned to use my magic, using my ability to predict fortunes just felt like what I was meant to do. Taking another breath in, I focused on trying to see what fortune awaited my friend.

Smoke filled the air and voices I didn't recognize shouted all around me. I couldn't understand what they said, but I caught sight of familiar uniforms. Ahn sat crouched down behind some debris, a gash on her forehead. Our gazes met and she whispered, "I'm sorry. I wasn't fast enough." In an instant the light went out of her eyes.

The vision faded as I scribbled down words to capture what I'd seen. I had never actually seen something like this unfold before when I'd used my power. Maybe it was such dire straits that the universe needed me to see it. I tried to go back through the short scene I'd witnessed, feeling for anything that felt like an intrusion or Tareq playing games. Nothing stood out that what I had seen wasn't true. I sat back, staring at the words I'd scrawled on the paper. Ahn hadn't looked much older than she did now, but what could have caused such destruction that would take her life? And more importantly, could I change it? I was across the room to where my friend sat, oblivious to what awaited her in the not-so-distant future. I couldn't help seeing the look of fear and sorrow she'd worn before she'd passed from this world. Whatever else was coming, facing Tareq was just the beginning.

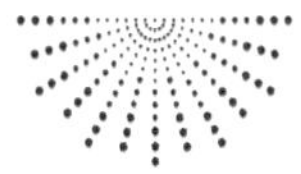

The minute I stepped out of my final exam, the walls around me vanished and I stood in the open fields just beyond the edge of campus. The wind whipped the hair out of Bashir's eyes and I could see the determination in them.

"I am here, shaqiq. Come and face me," Bashir called, his voice weary. He wanted this over as much as I did.

I wanted to move, but not being able to see my actual surroundings disoriented me. I'd never tried to break the connection with Bashir before, but I'd gotten what I needed from him. I knew where he was and that it was happening *now*.

'Let me go," I urged in his head.

Bashir's expression shifted from weary resoluteness to one of surprise, but the image faded and I was standing just beyond Dr. Shen's classroom.

"Are you okay, Mae Lin?" Ahn's voice came from directly behind me, making me jump.

"Yes. I can't really talk though. It's happening," I answered without looking at her. I couldn't face her, not with what I'd seen. I didn't trust my mind not to superimpose the look of her corpse over a still-living woman.

"Let us help," she called as I took off at a sprint.

"No time," I shouted back over my shoulder and thundered down the stairs.

Early summer air hit me in the face as I took off at a sprint across the grounds, casting a momentary glance toward the crypt. I hadn't seen Lee since our one encounter a few months ago, but I still got the impression he was hiding out. That was a problem for another day. My heart hammered painfully against my ribs and breastbone as I threw myself through the bushes.

Bashir stood alone on the hill when I skidded to a halt, using his arm to slow my forward momentum. I hadn't expected Tareq to wait until I'd arrived before attacking.

"How much time do we have?" I gasped, trying to bring my unruly lungs and heart under control.

"He's already here," Bashir answered.

I spun in a frantic circle, but saw no evidence to support his statement. We appeared to be alone. Then, at the bottom of the hill, I caught a flash of something vivid and red. It flickered as if he were teleporting a few steps at a time.

"I know how we can keep you and everyone safe," I said when it no longer hurt to breathe.

"I do not want you in this fight, Mae Lin. This is between my brother and me. And it will end with us."

"You aren't listening," I shouted, grabbing him by the shoulders and spinning him to face me. The sudden movement seemed to snap him out of his focus and he gave me an ashamed look.

"Do not think I say this because you are unskilled or lack power, but he murdered your grandmother and she had great power in her own right. If he could snuff out her life so easily, what makes you think you'll be any different?"

His words were harsh, but they didn't deter me. If anything, they fanned the flames of my desire to face Tareq head on and confront the man who had upended my life and thrown me into emotional chaos.

"At least let me try to protect you," I said, my hands already working as I spoke.

He couldn't deny me if I was already in the middle of casting the protective runes. Given that Tareq was already here, the invisibility rune seemed unnecessary, but I suspected I could link the lock rune with the protection rune just the same. I started by etching a protective barrier around us. The spell rippled out as far as I could see in all directions.

Pain sprang up behind my eyes at the amount of power it had taken to safeguard such a large space. I pushed it aside, turned to focus on Bashir and etched the lock and protection runes together.

"*Activas.*"

The magic flared fluorescent purple as it settled on Bashir. I watched him exhale, as if a weight had been lifted from his shoulders.

"You have done what you can, now go," Bashir begged me, giving me a hard shove back toward the school grounds.

I didn't have time to protest before Tareq was upon his brother. Despite the apparent age difference, I could still see how much they had once resembled one another except for the look in their eyes. Even if Bashir had aged as his brother had, I would never mistake him for his twin. The look in

Tareq's eyes was pure disgust and hatred—for me, for his brother.

Tareq lashed out, his hand claw-like and dragged away shards of purple light. I could see chinks in the magical armor I'd given Bashir, baring his vulnerable skin beneath it.

No, it was supposed to work.

It had seemed such a simple solution during the exam. Almost like a gift to face off against this monster. But here he was picking it apart with no more effort than if he were picking lint off an expensive suit.

"You waste her power," he snarled, looking at me over Bashir's left shoulder.

He needs to pay.

Anger cascaded over me, turning every nerve ending and sinew to fire within me. The feeling that had welled up within me that day months ago in Defensive Magic class returned and I prayed he hadn't dismantled enough of the protections I'd laid on Bashir as I let the wave of pure energy erupt outward. I could feel it press against the closer edges of the barrier, rebounding toward me. I couldn't stop it from hitting me and it knocked me off my feet.

Tareq's laughter filled my ears, the sound more

painful than anything I'd ever heard. I tried to cover my ears to block out the sound, but it did no good. The sound reverberated in my mind.

"You are a pale imitation of the woman whose power you pretend to wield," Tareq's voice taunted.

"Shut up," I ground through clenched teeth. "You do not get to talk about her like that."

I forced myself to my feet to face the man who was the root of so many troubles. He stood tall and triumphant as he hoisted Bashir high over his head with one hand. I could see the remains of the protection spell shattered on the ground around him.

In that moment, I couldn't stop from wondering what would happen to me if Bashir died while we were still connected. Would that be enough to sever our link? Or would it persist even in death? I had no desire to find out.

"You do not get to act as if you admired my grandmother when you murdered her all because she would not let you continue to hold an innocent man captive."

"Oh, how little you know of the woman you so idolize," Tareq sneered.

"I know you twisted everything and made her and O'Sullivan believe they had no other choice. But I also know she passed this gift on to me, so I could right that wrong. She saw through your lies in the end and I will not let you hurt him."

Tareq tossed Bashir to the ground at his feet. "Brave words, but your magic is no match for me."

He lazily sketched a rune in the air. I didn't even hear him utter the activation spell before I found myself flat on my back, arms spread out at my sides. I couldn't move and could barely breathe as he stood over me. He cocked his head to one side, studying me lying prone on the grass.

"I could take that power of yours, little Wisher," he taunted just as Bashir groaned and stirred behind him.

A jet of golden light snapped out from Bashir's palm, looped itself around Tareq's ankle and reeled it in like a fishing line. A little of the pressure keeping me immobilized lessoned as Tareq's attention diverted to his brother's attack. But not enough for me to do anything meaningful.

When Tareq turned back the smile on his lips looked like it had been carved with a wickedly sharp blade. "Let's see how strong you really are."

A pulse of red power leapt from his hands and into Bashir, whose body jerked as if hooked up to an electrical current. I wanted to shout at the man to stop, but the pain that jolted through my body stole my breath and my voice. Every ounce of pain Bashir felt came coursing through me. He was using our connection to toy with us and no matter what I felt under the surface, I couldn't fight back.

I could feel tears streaming down my cheeks as I tried not to bite through my own tongue in an effort to not scream in agony. The world around me began to grow grey out at the edges as Tareq's magic forced me toward the brink of unconsciousness.

I thought I heard someone yell my name in the distance. It didn't sound like Bashir's voice, but I couldn't move or look to see who'd called out. Something solid bumped my outstretched left hand and all of a sudden I could flex my fingers of my own accord. Tareq was busy torturing his brother, leaving an opening for a figure to scramble to my side and press the solid something into my hand. The figure leaned into my field of vision to reveal Lee.

"This is my fault. I have to try and help," he said just as Tareq spun back around and sent Lee hurtling into the barrier, landing on the ground with a concussive 'thud.' My fingers closed around what I now realized was the bit of Leprechaun luck. Risks be damned, I was going to use whatever I could to stop this maniac.

My hand tightened around the bit of gold and power coursed through me, freeing my body from Tareq's control. Even as he continued to pour power into Bashir, I no longer felt it. My luck wouldn't last long though. I couldn't explain how, but I could sense the object's power fading. Lee had probably used it all up. For a fleeting moment I worried about what would befall my father by using this bit of magic. He was the only living family I cared for. Ahn's face, pale and lifeless flashed before me and I shivered. Was I about to cause her death in the future?

"You ought to be careful with magic you don't understand," Tareq shouted, stopping his barrage on his brother to focus his attention on me.

Good, let him come for me.

"I understand well enough. It is a small risk compared to letting you roam free."

As I took a step forward, I noticed something shiny and pulsing coiled around Bashir's torso. It looked like a snake, its ethereal fangs latched on to his throat. He sputtered for air and his body now convulsed in time to the snake. Tareq may not want to kill his brother, but he clearly had no qualms about stealing magic that didn't belong to him. As Bashir tried to roll onto his back, I got a better look at the magic siphoning his power and realized it was a rune.

Just because my attempt to protect Bashir hadn't been effective, didn't mean I didn't understand how runes worked. Knowing what a rune symbolized and what it was meant to do was just as useful in casting a rune as in dismantling one.

I tried to recall what runes could siphon magic from a person, but none came to mind. The threat of the man standing before me didn't help. There was one rune that did come to mind and I sketched it hastily in the air in front of me before I whispered, "*Activas.*" As soon as I spoke the word, the air around me stilled and the pulsing of the spell latched on to Bashir stopped. The strain on his handsome features was paused mid-grimace. But it had worked, I had paused time. It would last maybe a few minutes.

That pain behind my eyes returned full force, causing double vision and nausea this time. I was throwing around more spells than I'd ever done before and my body was telling me in no uncertain terms it was a bad idea. Taking a shallow breath, I focused on the rune coiled around Bashir.

I still didn't recognize it and couldn't spend any more time on trying to decipher it. I hoped that reversing the direction of the lock rune and attaching it to the active spell would counteract the magic and free Bashir. But hoping wasn't enough. I still held the bit of gold in my hand.

"I don't know how this works, but if you've still got any power left, please help me save him," I whispered to the lump of metal.

It grew warm in my hand as I sketched the inverse of the lock rune, making sure it attached to the snake at the mouth positioned around Bashir's throat.

"*Activas.*"

A high-pitched shrieking filled my ears as a rush of magic knocked me back onto my butt in the grass. Bashir's body still sat at an unnatural angle mid-convulsion, but the snake had disappeared.

Time resumed its normal course at the same time and Tareq whirled to see that I'd freed his brother. Still, Bashir didn't appear to be in any condition to fight back. At least not without some help.

Every inch of my body ached to the bone, but I pushed it aside. My hands acted of their own volition, sketching runes strung together before my brain could catch up and decipher their meaning. I pushed them toward Bashir as I uttered a hoarse *"Activas."*

Bashir glowed, rising to his feet like a marionette. He opened his eyes and they blazed vibrant gold as did every inch of his skin. I could see Tareq taking a step back as Bashir advanced, hands held up in fists. Whether he intended to sling magic from them or just use them was beyond my comprehension.

"You always wanted us to be stronger than anyone. I believe you have finally had your wish come true." Bashir's voice echoed in the barrier that still managed to stay untouched.

"You locked me away in the hopes of beating me. Your plans have failed. I should grant you no mercy, no shred of decency. But you are my brother and no matter the horrors you have heaped on me, I find I still love you."

"Love is for the weak. You would be a fool to let me live, brother," Tareq snarled.

"Then you will face justice for your crimes," Bashir answered and power rippled off his skin like steam and sought to bind his brother in chains forged solely of Djinn magic. But I spotted hints of purple laced in the energy coiling around each finger. My essence was giving him strength to face his brother. I was helping after all.

Out of the corner of my eye, I could see the barrier begin to fade as my energy and ability to stay conscious wavered. It was enough for Tareq's magic to flare and transport him out of Bashir's reach.

I wanted to move, to make sure that both Bashir and Lee were unharmed, but I couldn't get my body to follow simple commands. I only had enough energy to keep my eyes open and see Bashir lean over me.

"You are going to be okay," he said, his voice sounding a million miles off.

I wanted to nod, but even that was too much effort. I swallowed, my throat raw and whispered. "Get Lee."

"Rest now. You did wonderfully," Bashir whispered, scooping me up in his arms.

"He got away," I mumbled, my head resting in the crook of his shoulder and neck.

"Our fight was not meant to end here. But you must rest now," he insisted and I could sense the weight of his words.

I longed to protest, but my eyes refused to stay open any longer. The pain I'd endured at Tareq's hands combined with the overuse of my magic had wiped me out completely.

I had enough awareness to worry for a moment about what would happen if he breached the security on the grounds, but it wasn't enough of a concern to tether me to the land of the waking. I listened to Bashir's footsteps as he carried me back to safety and the world around me vanished into darkness.

CHAPTER NINETEEN

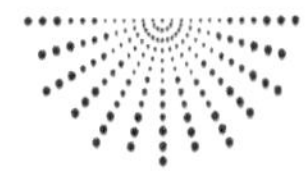

My ears rang as I came to in the medical wing of the school. I was beginning to hate this place and the fact I ended up here far too often at the end of term. I sat up against the pillows and saw Siobhan with Ahn sitting by my bedside. Thankfully, my new friend looked no worse for wear and my mind had compartmented what I'd seen during the exam away for now. Whatever fate I'd seen for her, it was still far enough in the future maybe we could do something to change things.

"This is a normal thing for you, huh?" Ahn noted when she saw I was awake.

"Unfortunately, I can't say it isn't," I sighed, massaging the left side of my head. I had vague recollections of hitting it when Tareq had sent me sprawling right before he'd begun his torture of ...

Bashir!

I closed my eyes and focused, trying to call an image of him into my mind. The odd tingling sensation I'd started to associate with our connection remained, humming along just below the surface of our magic. I had to believe that meant he was still alive. But then the memory of him carrying me back to the grounds resurfaced.

"You want to tell us what happened? Because I'm not going to forgive you for a long time for going off without us," Siobhan said, arms crossed over her chest in displeasure.

"I didn't have time. Bashir sent me a vision that he was luring Tareq to a fight and I had to be there," I answered. "If it makes you feel better, I don't think we've seen the last of Tareq."

"I would have to agree with you on that, Ms. Zhou," Dr. O'Sullivan's voice rang out from a few beds down.

I sat up straighter as he approached and picked up on the sound of two sets of footsteps. I studied the older man's expression. It reflected a healthy dose of guilt and shame as the second figure stepped around him and a wave of relief surged through me.

"You're okay," I addressed Bashir as he came to sit on the side of the bed.

"Thanks to you," he answered, giving my hand a squeeze.

I eyed O'Sullivan. "I don't understand. How is he here? And how do you know he's here?"

"Contrary to your belief, I do know most of what goes on at this school."

"But wouldn't he have set off the security measures?"

"Oh, I did. You were unconscious when we arrived and there were many guards. But Ronan was gracious enough to call them off when he realized you were in need of medical attention," Bashir answered.

I looked to O'Sullivan. "You spent all this time thinking Bashir was the enemy. Why change your mind now?"

O'Sullivan sighed, averting his gaze. "I will admit that my involvement in Bashir's internment was shameful and I regret my actions. But I see now that the true threat was always Tareq. I let him convince me and your grandmother that we were protecting people, when in reality, we were imprisoning our best chance at defending this school."

"You think he's going to come after the school?"

"I saw it in his mind while we fought. He wants to destroy the school and rebuild it in his own image. Only allow Djinn in. I could see his desire to strip magic from Wishers and Leprechauns, too."

I didn't want to think about what that meant. I was just grateful that Bashir was alive and appeared to have recovered from the ill effects of his brother's magical assaults. Now we had time to formulate a defense plan to keep the school safe. I turned back to Dr. O'Sullivan. "Lee was there. He tried to help. Is he … what happened to him?"

"Mr. Wu is convalescing a few beds down from you. Given his actions, we are willing to readmit him for classes in the fall." O'Sullivan cast one look over his shoulder before adding, "I will give him credit for being resourceful, although I do not condone his use of Leprechaun magic to escape the wards on the grounds and will be holding him accountable. I do not appreciate students making a mockery of the measures I've put in place to protect them."

I exhaled a breath I hadn't been aware I was holding before looking to Bashir. "Is that okay with you, if he comes back to school?"

"I understand his motivations. Family is a complicated matter regardless of one's magical background. I hold no ill will toward him. Although, selfish as it sounds, I am grateful that if I had to be bound to anyone, it was to you."

My cheeks burned in embarrassment at his attempt to flirt with me.

"I do hope you will be feeling up to joining everyone for the end of semester party," Dr. O'Sullivan said, looking to each of us in turn.

"We'll see you down there in a bit," Siobhan said and ushered Ahn away.

The space grew quiet and I tried to listen for anyone else rustling about beneath bedsheets, but heard nothing. It was then I spotted the tiny runes etched into the floor glowing a soothing shade of dandelion yellow—silencing runes.

"This has been a really long year," I said, falling back against the pillows.

"You have handled it marvelously and I know that your grandmother would be proud of you," Bashir offered.

"But we're no closer to finding out how to break the bond between us. We know it had to do with the fact I wished you free and it's probably linked to the fact my bloodline was involved in the spell that bound you originally."

"We have time to unravel all of those mysteries. But for now, be grateful that we are both alive and recovering from my brother's attacks. It will be nice to join you for the festivities properly this year."

"No more sneaking around," I noted.

"Not anymore. And you will get your wish. I have spoken with Ronan and we have come to an arrangement that I will return for my final year in the fall alongside your class."

"I thought everything was still too fresh for you to be on campus," I replied. "Not that I'm not excited to see you here."

"I believe that my place is here by your side. You were right. Finding answers will be easier when we are together. And this way, I know that I will be close by if Tareq tries to use this bond against us like he did this time."

"I like that idea," I said and reached for his hand, squeezing it tight. "I'm sorry he caused you such pain. I can't imagine inflicting that kind of agony on someone who is my flesh and blood."

"I am only sorry you had to feel it, too. But you gave me more strength than I thought possible," Bashir replied. "For that, I am grateful."

"I don't know how I knew what to do."

"There comes a time where you either know the material or you do not," he said, parroting my words to Ahn before our Wish Craft exam and I smiled. "I guess I did know more than I realized."

He flashed me another smile and it was the most free I'd ever seen him. There was danger ahead, but in this moment, all he saw was the joy of being alive and being together.

It was infectious and I put all of the fear of the things I'd seen out of my mind. "Come on. Let's go down and join everyone."

After stopping by the dorm to change, we headed for the first floor to find most of the first-year students crowded around the exam results. I waited until there was a gap in the crowd to slip in and search for my name. I found my results quick enough. Good I'd passed everything and that was all I needed to know. I did smile a little bigger as I noted the A in Runes. Dr. Corbitt would no doubt be seeing me in his advanced class come September.

Bashir and I walked outside and spotted Siobhan and Ahn lounging by a tree. As we got food and joined them, I couldn't shake the feeling that I was forgetting something. That something was just a little off kilter.

"What is on your mind?" Bashir whispered in my ear.

"I don't know. Something feels off. I didn't notice

it while we were in the infirmary, but out here, it's more noticeable. Like I'm off balance."

I turned my focus inward. I could still feel my magic coiled in my core, ready to spring to life. But when I tried to coax it to do my bidding, it was sluggish, almost confused by what I wanted it to do. *That isn't good.* Raising my hands to the air around me, I etched the first actual rune I'd ever used.

"Activas."

The spell enveloped me, drawing the attention of my friends as the mist that swirled within the confines was a vibrant shimmering gold with only the tiniest hints of purple.

"What happened to my magic?"

QUICK AUTHOR'S NOTE

WERE you surprised by the fact that we finally got the answer to who killed Mae Lin's grandmother, and why? When I was originally writing this, I didn't quite realize just what the murder meant (I know, you'd think I would given that I'm the one writing this story, but sometimes the characters do their own thing, or new ideas come to fruition as I write).

I knew it was important to not only show Mae Lin's growth with her powers, but also set up a few final nuggets of story threads for her to unravel in the final book. What do you think happened to her magic at the end?

I LIKED BEING able to explore some more practical classes in this story, especially Runes. I don't know why but I'm rather fascinated by it as a subject and the way it interacts in academy stories. And hey, it happens to prove useful in the end!

SPEAKING of what's coming next, our villain may be laying low for a little while, but his presence will be felt far more within the academy itself in the final installment. And Mae Lin will be forced to work with people she'd much rather avoid.

TURN the page to get a sneak peek at *Luck Changer*.

Wishing for the past just might reveal the future...

Mae Lin Zhou returns for her final year at Kismet Academy even more lost than when she first arrived. Fearing her magic is irreversably altered, she faces battles from within and without as she struggles to understand the weakened magic now flowing in her veins.

As students begin losing their magic, Mae Lin vows to remaster her magic. Relying on old friends, trusted allies and frenemies, she just might have a chance to defend the place has become her home.

When the final fight inevitably comes crashing through the school's gates, will Mae Lin be able to face down the man who started on this magical journey? Or will she be his next victim in his quest for power and glory?

Read on for a glimpse as Mae Lin's final chapter...

ABOUT THE AUTHOR

Sarah Biglow is a *USA Today* bestselling author. She lives in Massachusetts with her husband and son. She is a licensed attorney and spends her days combatting employment discrimination as an Investigator with the Massachusetts Commission Against Discrimination.

You can find an up-to-date list of all my books here